She Said It's
Your Child

She Said It's Your Child

Sherene Holly Cain

www.urbanbooks.net

Urban Books, LLC
300 Farmingdale Road, NY-Route 109
Farmingdale, NY 11735

She Said It's Your Child

ISBN 13: 978-1-60162-907-4
ISBN 10: 1-60162-907-9

First Trade Paperback Printing May 2019
Printed in the United States of America

10 9 8 7 6 5 4 3 2 1

*This is a work of fiction. Any references or similarities
to actual events, real people, living or dead, or to real
locales are intended to give the novel a sense of reality.
Any similarity in other names, characters, places, and
incidents is entirely coincidental.*

Distributed by Kensington Publishing Corp.
Submit Orders to:
Customer Service
400 Hahn Road
Westminster, MD 21157-4627
Phone: 1-800-733-3000
Fax: 1-800-659-2436

Acknowledgments

All thanks, honor, and glory to God. With you, all things are possible.

To my children and biggest fans, Demetri, I'munique, and Shameek Stephens (grandson Shane Stephens). My heart beats for you and words cannot express how much you mean to me.

To my loving husband, Darrell Cain, for his undying love and support. You are my rock. I love you more than life.

To the best sister in the universe, Angela Bennett, for all you do; it would take me too long to list. I love you past infinity.

To my brother, Chris Naulls, for loving the work I do and letting me know often.

To Aunties Alma Mock, Darlene Fontenot, Gloria Baker, and Deborah Baker. Cousins Janell, Neisha, Raylecia, Raycinta, Cathy, Shonnyce, Jackie, Donnicka; Sisters Chea, Olivia, Babylisa, Brenda, and Kitten for making sure I know my worth.

Thanks, Uncle Raymond, Ernest, Donovan, and Duane for letting me borrow your strength during the difficult times.

Thank you, Mama Gwen Baker and Daddy Sammie Holly, Grandpa Ernest G. Baker Sr., and my dear husband Donald Ray Stephens. RIP, loves.

To Torica, my publisher, mentor, and friend. Thanks, love. I hope you know that you're the best.

Acknowledgments

Thanks to my Torica Tymes Presents family, especially Rae Zellous and Chenell Parker who continue to support my efforts and promote my books.

Margaret Flack, no one in the world can compare to you, and I mean that from the bottom of my heart. Thanks.

Elle Welch, I want to thank you for being so special, so talented, and so lovely. Don't change.

Johnazia Gray, I love you so much, my beautiful and spirited twin. Thanks.

To Keyla (Keys) Anderson, my sister and still one of my biggest fans. Your support is better than diamonds.

To Michelle Neal, Earline Hamell, Regina Mathis-Pollack, and Kendra Huskey, always rooting for me, and I appreciate it to the fullest. Thank you.

Viola King, because you are such a gift, I'm praying continuously for yours.

To my diva, JM Hart, thanks for always being there with feedback and support.

Thanks, Sherry Boose, for being such a supportive and real reader.

Thank you, David Weaver, Cole Hart, and Torica Tymes, for being the forerunners and groundbreakers of this movement and for blessings to so many.

To my sisters with the biggest hearts and most beautiful smiles in the world, Genesis Woods and Jessica Wren. Keep it coming.

Thanks, Sherene's Dream members for the love and support you continue to show me whenever I need it, any time, day or night.

Thanks, Author Mopain Taylor, for the help and encouragement you continue to provide me. Love ya.

Thanks to my beautiful editor La'Shan Michele because she is truly a talented and dedicated soul.

Last but not least, thanks to all my readers. You make it worth all the work.

Dedication 1

This book is dedicated to all the single parents who sacrifice daily to make sure their children have food on the table and also to the women and men who are not biological parents but continuously bring the gift of love to so many children who need it.

Dedication 2

This book is dedicated to my uncle, Ernest Baker Jr., whose untimely death happened while I was finishing this book. You brought light into my life when I needed it the most and made a drastic impact on me. I wasn't planning on you leaving so soon, but I guess God needed another angel to keep him company in heaven. RIP, Uncle Popo. See you at the next "family reunion."

Follow me on Facebook: Sherene Holly Cain,
or Author Sherene, or Author Sherene II

Twitter: Sherene2009

Instagram: Sherene Holly Cain

Email: enerehs2008@yahoo.com

Goodreads: Sherene Holly Cain

Amazon Central: Sherene Holly Cain

Books by Sherene Holly Cain

Try Sleeping with a Broken Heart 1, 2, 3, and 4

The Way That I Love Him

I Can't Make You Love Me

Ring the Alarm

Beard Gang Chronicles I and III

Chapter One

Rolanda

Thanksgiving 1989

I woke up at six o'clock in the morning to Brandon sucking on my right breast. "Oh my God, baby. What are you doing?"

"You're definitely about to find out," he stopped long enough to say, then went right to work on my left nipple.

"Damn, baby," I moaned. He pushed two fingers inside my sinewy walls and fingered me until they were soaking wet. "Ummmmmmmm. You're getting me hot," I said as I backed away. He grabbed my legs and pulled my lower lips close to his mouth.

"I need you boiling," he said.

"Baby, nooooo!" I screamed. "I have to cook." Brandon ignored my protests as he feasted on my swollen clit and ate me like I was his last meal. "Ooooooooh, baaaaaby," I screamed. "That feels so good." My eyes rolled to the back of my head, and I started thrashing against his tongue. "Pleeeeeeeeeease," I begged.

"Please what?" he interrupted his foreplay long enough to ask. I knew he was going in for the kill because he started sucking and licking my love button for dear life. He flipped me over, and I straddled his mouth until I had the most mind-blowing orgasm that left me shaking like a leaf. Brandon wiped the remnants of my juices off his chin and allowed me to come down from the roller-coaster ride he just took me on, but I could tell he wasn't done with me.

"Get ready for part two," he announced before putting my legs on his strong shoulders and filling me up with his thick rod. I closed my eyes and succumbed to the pleasure only he could give me.

I didn't get Thanksgiving dinner started until seven thirty, and I was running around the kitchen like a chicken with my head cut off, trying to chop up the onions, celery, and bell peppers for my dressing and potato salad. I boiled the noodles for my macaroni and cheese, washed my greens, rubbed my turkey with seasonings, and placed it in the oven. Then I got dressed. By the time I finished, it was nine o'clock in the morning, and Brandon was still asleep. I guess he was tired from all the sex.

By two o'clock, my dinner was done. I stood back to admire my handiwork. I was glad I pulled this off since Mama C wasn't here for me to consult with, and she, unfortunately, wouldn't be here to celebrate.

At the age of 16, two years ago, I left home in love and pregnant with Brandon's baby. Mama hated him.

"He's no good, and he's never going to amount to anything," she told me.

"He's not like the rest of the thugs in our hood that sell crack to everybody, including their own mama. At least he works," I bragged. I actually thought I did good finding a man.

"At your age, you have no idea what life is about," she said. "Brandon's got your nose wide open. He's the first man whose kisses made you feel like the luckiest woman in the world, and I can only imagine what else he's done to you."

What she didn't know, and I would never tell her was Brandon made me come so hard, my body shook like a human earthquake. Plus, he was so fine; every woman that laid eyes on him wanted a taste of his white chocolate. I felt blessed to have him. "If you let him trick you into leaving this house, you can forget about coming back," she added. Shortly after I left, I found out why Mama hated him so much. She knew he would hurt me.

I was a beautiful woman with a sexy body before and after I got pregnant. I had high cheekbones, long, natural hair, creamy caramel skin, big beautiful breasts, wide hips, and long, sexy legs. When I walked down the street in my flower pants and tight blouse, every man in the city of Belle took notice.

The day I met Brandon, I was coming from the corner store when a group of guys started whistling at me. I laughed and kept walking, but one of them called out to me.

"Damn, baby. You working them flower pants!" he yelled from his Nissan truck.

I turned around to cuss him out for disrespecting me, but I looked into warm, brown eyes and dimples, and I was speechless. He had on his work uniform and badge, and it read "Belle Sanitation." He may have been driving around with his homeboys, but I knew he was in a whole different league. He was making an honest living; plus, he was fine.

I took a long look at the handsome specimen and found more reasons to love him. He had waves for days, and if it wasn't for the high top fade, I would've thought he was mixed. I usually didn't go for light skin, but his complexion was smooth and clear, his features were picture-perfect, he was all tatted up, and he had muscles for days. He jumped out of the truck and started walking toward me. Dayum, I licked my lips. This tall drink of water had the nerve to be bow-legged.

"Hi. My name is Brandon. What's yours?"

"Rolanda."

"Nice to meet you, Rolanda. Did you know you were over here stopping traffic?"

"Really?"

"Yeah. I almost crashed."

"I bet you say that to all the ladies."

"I never met a lady like you. I have to get to know you. Can you write down your phone number for me?"

I rummaged in my purse for a pen, but he already had one ready, so I gave him my number without hesitation. We were inseparable after that and fell into a routine of watching movies and eating dinner together at my house on week nights and taking in a movie or hanging out at his place on weekends.

On the days we didn't see each other, he called me, and we talked until one of us fell asleep, and we woke up at the crack of dawn on the telephone saying good morning to each other.

It only took three months for him to get me pregnant and another for Mama to notice my baby bump. She was mad as hell, but she had no choice but to accept it and help me all she could. Her only rules were, "Make sure you finish school and don't bring Brandon in my house when I'm not here."

It sounded pretty easy at the time but turned out to be short-lived. Not only did Brandon come over while Mama was gone, but he also had me bent over the bed screaming out his name on a regular basis. Mama came home early one day because she had a head cold and couldn't finish her shift. She heard us having sex, and the next thing we knew, she was beating on my door.

"Ro, you better get that lowlife out of my house before I shoot his ass!" she screamed.

I put on a robe and came out with my head held down in shame, but Brandon came out proudly zipping his pants.

He gave Mama a cocky stare. "Pack your stuff, Ro. You're moving with me," he looked at me and said.

I packed as much as I could into a Hefty bag and walked out the door as Mama issued her threats.

My first night at Brandon's house was rocky. I was worried sick about Mama because I left home so suddenly. I knew she was probably calling Brandon every name in the book by now because she was worried about me. This was my first time away from Mama, and even though I was pregnant with a child of my own, I felt scared and alone. I loved Brandon more than anything in the world, but I was torn between the two.

Brandon fixed up the house nice, and it felt like home. We spent the day making love and only stopped to eat and drink water. It was the closest thing to heaven I'd ever felt . . . until our visitor showed up.

It was about nine o'clock in the evening, and we were exhausted from our afternoon romp and dead asleep when we heard someone banging on the door. Brandon jumped up, bolted out of bed, and ran to the door.

"You man enough to lie down and make a baby, but you can't take care of it?" a woman yelled.

"Get the hell off my porch!" he barked.

She threw a rock at the bedroom window, causing it to crack.

"What the hell is going on, Brandon?" I sat up in bed and screamed.

"Nothing. That was my crazy neighbor. I'm sorry she woke you up, baby. Go back to sleep."

I eyed him suspiciously, then lay down and followed his orders. The "disgruntled neighbor" never showed up again, but our phone was ringing off the hook every night for a week. Brandon always answered and hung up on whoever it was.

My trip down memory lane ended when Brandon walked into the kitchen with his boys, Stevie and Trae. "Um, um, um, baby. You got it smelling good in here!" he exclaimed.

"Thanks. Dinner is ready," I said as several more of his friends came in. I got so busy fixing plates and socializing that I didn't notice I was hungry until I heard my stomach growling. I fixed a big plate of food, brought it to the living room, and started eating. The next thing I knew, Brandon was walking up to me and introducing me to a young girl who was around 16 years old.

"This my sister, Landi," he said.

I reached my hand out to shake hers, but she made no effort to extend hers. I eyed her in disbelief. Brandon had introduced me to his mother and two brothers but had clearly missed mentioning or introducing me to his sister. I wanted to ask him where the hell she had been, what side of the family was she from, why they didn't look like each other, and had they gotten mixed up at birth, but everyone in the house got real quiet, and I didn't want to make a big scene.

I struggled to see a family resemblance between them, but I definitely didn't miss her big belly. She looked extremely uncomfortable, like she was trying to find an escape route and barely nodded, let alone greeted me. Brandon fixed her a plate. She didn't say a word to anyone as she picked at her food.

Toward the end of the evening when everyone was leaving, she was still sitting on our couch. I didn't bother to talk to her rude ass because she did not attempt to socialize. I thought the wench suffered from mental illness or some speech impediment.

"Landi got evicted and don't have nowhere to go," Brandon mumbled. "I told her she can sleep on our sofa tonight."

"Why would you do that without asking me first? I don't like her attitude."

"Don't be selfish, Ro. It's Thanksgiving."

"We fed her and kept her out of the cold. That's charity enough."

"Baby, it's just for one night."

"Fine," I said as I stomped away and prepared for bed.

At around one in the morning, I went to the bathroom and decided to pass by the kitchen on my way back to bed. I heard the voices of Brandon and his boys as they were playing cards.

"When I grow up, I want to be like my boy, B," Stevie said, referring to Brandon.

"Why do you say that?" Brandon asked curiously.

"You got two fine-ass bitches under the same roof. You planning a threesome?" he blurted. Brandon looked around to make sure no one was listening.

"Keep it down, man. Ro will kill me if she finds out."

I couldn't believe what I just heard. It made me feel sick and stupid at the same time, but I didn't say anything to Brandon. I ran into the living room to confront Landi, who slept soundly on our couch.

"Wake up," I shoved her. Landi rubbed her eyes and sat up.

"What?" she spoke for the first time in twelve hours.

"You pregnant with Brandon's baby?"

"No."

"Don't lie."

"I didn't want to come. It was Brandon's idea. I was going to sleep on a park bench after I got kicked out. He made me do this," she whined.

I didn't stick around to hear the rest of her rant. I was too busy racing into the kitchen to confront Brandon.

"Why did you bring that girl to my house?"

"The last time I checked, you wasn't working or paying for shit. This is *my* house, and I can bring whoever I want in here. I told you it was just for one night."

"You lied. She's pregnant by you."

"I didn't mean to knock her up. It was a mistake, baby."

"I guess next you're going to tell me she slipped and fell on your dick."

"Can you get Landi a room?" Brandon asked Stevie as he handed him a twenty-dollar bill.

"No problem, man," Stevie said as he looked at me with guilty eyes.

I shook my head as he and Landi hurriedly walked out the back door. Then I scrambled to pack up my son's and my belongings.

"Where are you going? I got rid of her like you wanted me to."

"Fuck you, Brandon. You should never have brought her here in the first place."

Before I could get any more words out of my mouth, he grabbed me by the neck, cutting off my air supply. When I clawed at his hands to get him to release me, he pushed me on the ground, grabbed a belt, and started swinging it at me, causing welts to form on my caramel flesh.

"Your ass, *whack,* ain't going, *whack,* nowhere, *whack!* You belong, *whack,* to me, *whack!*"

I tried to get up and run, but he kicked me repeatedly.

"Nooooo! Let me go!" I begged. I gave him a run for his money, grabbing his foot and making him fall to the ground. Then I scratched the heck out of his face and punched him as hard as I could. But my little fists were no match for Brandon, who was now at the point of no return. He punched me in the head, back, and arms until

I was black and blue. I eventually realized I was losing the battle and gave up the fight, using my arms to cover my head.

By the time he was finished with me, I had a black eye, a swollen upper lip, and a bloody bottom one. My skin had scrapes, scratches, lumps, and whip marks. When he was tired of beating me, he looked at me, shook his head, and went to bed like nothing ever happened. Luckily for me, my son had spent the night with my cousin. I took whatever I could, once again, in a trash bag and headed to the only place I knew to go. When I arrived, I beat on her door for dear life.

"What the hell's going on?" Mama C screamed when she heard me assault her door.

"Sorry. I didn't have anywhere else to go," I cried.

"Come in," she said.

I walked into her house for the first time in two years and felt love all over me. Except for some new curtains and some throw pillows, not much had changed. The smell of turkey and greens wafted from the kitchen like it did every Thanksgiving, and when she closed the door behind me, I felt safe.

Mama hated Brandon so much that she had refused to visit me while I was living with him. But she kept in touch with me over the phone, visited her grandson at my cousin's house, and even babysat him sometimes. She invited me over for dinner often, but I was too ashamed to step foot in her house. So, I stayed home with Brandon most of the time.

"That son of a bitch put his hands on you again," she spat.

"How do you know this isn't the first time?"

"I've been on this earth long enough to know. You leaving him for good this time?"

"Yeah."

"Forget what I said about not being welcome to come back. I'm not sending you back to that bastard, baby."

"Thanks, Mama," I said as I embraced her. "But I need to get away from here for a while. I want to leave Brandon and never look back."

"Do what you have to do, baby. But there's always a better way to deal with things. I just want you to know that running is the easiest thing to do but not always the smartest."

Chapter Two

Nolan 2014

"I've been trying to get rid of her for sixteen hours," I told my half brother, Greg. He laughed so loud that I had to take the phone off my ear.

"What you want me to do? Come over there and pry her off you?" he asked.

"After I blew her back out a few times, I thought for sure she'd be running out of here."

"See, that's where you messed up. You should have took her to a room or went to her place."

"If I would've known she was this hard to get rid of, trust and believe, I never would have invited her over. My head is hurting, and I'm dehydrated, and she keeps rambling about how much fun we had."

"Tell her ass all good things must come to an end and show her the door. You don't go to somebody's house, fuck the shit out of them, and then start planning a future. At some point, you go home, especially since that's where all your clothes are."

"Don't get me wrong, Mina is a nice girl, but she talks too much, she's sexually insatiable and greedy as all get-out. I fed her dinner, dessert, breakfast, and a snack, and she's *still* hungry. If she ain't eating me out of house and home, she's sucking on me like a protein shake. You don't just dive on a man and milk him dry whenever you feel the urge."

"Looks like you finally met your match," Greg teased.

"Her greedy butt can forget it. As much as I love sex and food, I'm not cooking another thing, and I'm damn sure not taking my pants off again."

"I thought you said feeding and fucking women, not exactly in that order, was your favorite pastime."

"Yeah, I did. You know I have a healthy appetite in both areas, and I please them on both counts. But even I have my limits."

"People always said you was easy on the eyes and a healer by nature. I guess you laid them hands on her so good that it finally caught up with you."

My brother was right. I went to school to be a doctor and got a job at one of the most prestigious hospitals in the country, Lake Hospital, where I'd been employed for two years. But, some people said I missed my calling because I looked more like a model or an actor. Even the nurses who saw me save lives didn't believe it at times. I guess that's why I worked so hard at my job. My boss recognized my skills early on and elevated me to head surgeon.

"This ain't nothing compared to what happened at the hospital when I first started working there. I messed up big time when I slept with some of the staff. I had nurses, receptionists, and doctors cornering me in hallways, broom closets, offices, and bathrooms, trying to get a first or second taste of my so-called perfect dick. One nurse came at me right in front of a patient."

"Hey, Doctor Feelgood," she said.

"Excuse me?" I asked.

"Or should I call you Mr. Fill Her and Heal Her, Medicine Man, or Doctor Dickmatize."

"You need to chill," I warned her.

"What's the matter? You don't like your nicknames?"

I excused myself from the patient's room and walked out to the hallway. The nurse followed me all the way to the parking lot.

"Let's do it right here." She pointed to my Ferrari.

"Against my car?"

"Yes."

"No thanks," I declined.

"Then, unzip your pants and let me take you to heaven," she said as she got on her knees.

"Hell no," I spat. Even if it wasn't broad daylight, I wasn't about to indulge her vulgar ass. Women say men are nasty, but they take the cake. There was a serial killer rumored to be walking around on the hospital grounds, but the only thing that mattered to most of the women at Lake was getting laid.

"I want to see if all the rumors are true," she stated.

I didn't bother to ask what she meant because I knew what they were saying about me.

"I heard you have a dick that most men would kill for."

In my opinion, I just knew how to work it well.

"I heard you have a magic tongue too," she added.

I just felt like my tongue game was above average. I got approached about it a lot, but most of the time, I declined. Don't get me wrong; I loved eating as much as they loved receiving, but putting my mouth on everyone was something I just didn't do. They had to meet my standards.

"I'm not having sex with you, so go on back in the hospital before I report you for sexual harassment and abandoning patients."

"You have a lot of nerve," she huffed as she adjusted her uniform and walked back toward the hospital.

Everybody I slept with believed that she was the one, and when I didn't want anything to do with them after that, they got mad. I hadn't met a female yet who could resist me or walk away from me. I wasn't planning on getting married or looking to fall in love, but women found that hard to accept. I'd only been in love once and wasn't planning on doing it again anytime soon. I honestly didn't think the right woman would ever come along.

"All I can say, brother, is I wish I had your problems."

"You mean, in addition to your wife and mistress?"

"The more, the merrier," he laughed. "I'll catch you later, man."

"Cool," I said as I hung up my phone.

I saw that my brother, Dolan, had called more than ten times. I wanted to get back to him, but I needed to get a handle on this situation first. Dolan and I had a rocky relationship, but we always managed to work it out. Lately, we'd been trying to bond, mostly because our parents hated us to be at odds with each other. We really did want to put everything behind us once and for all, since half of the stuff we beefed about was silly. I hoped he didn't think I was ignoring him. I was anxious to talk to him.

I didn't know much about our real dad, except that he was also blessed with good looks and stamina. My mother was a beauty and had men running after her too. I guess they deserved the credit for the attention I was getting.

Another call came through, and I knew it was Evette without even looking. She'd been blowing my phone up all day because she wanted to spend some quality time with me too. I knew she was probably wondering why I wasn't responding to her. I'd known her for a while, and I could count on one hand the number of times I wasn't available when she really needed me.

Evette was spoiled, but she knew by now that I wouldn't get to her until I was good and ready, and when I did, she might not like what I had to say. If I wanted to spend my off day with her, I would have called her this morning. As for Mina, she was on her way out the door.

"You okay, baby?" Mina asked worriedly.

"Yeah. I think I have a hunger headache," I said as I massaged my temples.

"You want me to fix you something to eat or get you some Tylenol, daddy?"

"I'm cool." *The last time I ate your food, I got sick,* I said to myself.

"Too bad you're not feeling well. I was about to put it on you," she grinned.

"I'm just going to lay it down," I said, hoping Mina would take the hint and leave. But she planted herself on my bed to let me know that was the last thing on her mind. *That's it,* I thought to myself. *I need to take matters into my own hands.*

"I enjoyed your company, love, but I'm on call, and my boss told me I have to go to work in an hour."

"I can stay here until you get off," she offered.

"No thanks. I have to do a long shift at the hospital, and I don't want to leave you here by yourself."

A look of disappointment washed over Mina's face, and she started biting her nails like a kid, knowing how much I hated it. If she had shown any signs of that freaky habit when I met her, she never would've made the cut. I guess she didn't catch my hints that I wanted her to get a manicure or at least file them down.

"The next time I see you, I'm taking you to the nail shop to get you some French tips."

"It's a date, daddy. I can't wait."

It was funny; when I offered to pay for her to get them done on her own, her ass didn't take me up on my offer.

Now that she saw it as an opportunity to spend some time with me, she jumped right on it.

"OK, let me know when you get home. We have a lot of unfinished business to take care of," she said.

The last thing I wanted to do, after three or four surgeries, was play with Mina again. I didn't care how horny I got, I would jack off before I called her. She'd be lucky to get another invite in the next month or so. Her time to exit was past due.

I tossed her a towel and washcloth to speed things along. She gave me the evil eye, ran into the bathroom, and slammed the door like her ass was crazy. I heard her abuse the shower door too. It sounded like she snatched the shit right off the hinges. Her lack of respect for my property was pissing me off. She came out of the bathroom huffing, stomping, and glaring at me while she got dressed like I was going to change my mind or something. After that slamfest she just had, the chances of that were slim to none.

I breathed a sigh of relief when she walked past me without so much as good riddance and closed the main door with a final bang. I locked it and leaned up against it. Evette was calling right on cue, so I decided to give her the same excuse.

"Hey, doll. I can't meet you tonight. I have to work."

"Damn, baby. I really need to spend some quality time with you," she whined.

"I want that too," I lied. "Maybe we can get together later."

"I hope so. I miss you so much—" she started to say.

I hung up the phone before she got the words out and was already on my next project, turning last night's leftovers into a chicken breast salad. The meal was complete in twenty minutes and smelled delicious. I scooped up a forkful and was about to dig in when my phone rang. I put my lunch on hold to answer the call.

"Hello."

"Hey, man!" my brother yelled. "I've been looking all over for you. Where the hell have you been?"

"Hey, bruh. Sorry. I was entertaining one of my honeys. She had me in a headlock."

"You're a mess, man. That's why I'm married. I don't need those problems."

"You want to grab a drink later?"

"Yeah. Meet me at Massey's. Darica is on one, and I know she won't be nothing nice."

"Trouble in paradise?"

"It's a little more complicated than that," Dolan laughed.

"Well, it looks like you could use some advice from your big brother."

"I don't know about all that, man. You ain't that much older than me."

"See you after work, bruh."

"Okay."

Dolan 2014

After disconnecting the phone call with Nolan, I looked in the lobby to see how many clients were left. Thank God, there was only one. After staying late all week and taking on twice as much work, I was exhausted. My boss was thankful for my help and promised to give me a bonus once we got the busy office under control. But to be honest, I wanted nothing more than a getaway, alone with my beautiful wife.

"Hello. My name is Dolan. I'll be assisting you today," I greeted the lone customer in the waiting room.

"It's nice to meet you, Dolan. I'm Tonette. Sorry, I forgot most of my documents." She had on a halter top and shorts that left little to the imagination. Her full breasts were spilling over, and her huge butt was peeking out.

You forgot most of your outfit too, I thought. "No problem. I can show you how to pull up the information on the company website."

"Dayum. You sure you're supposed to be working here?" she asked.

I nodded as I asked, "Why?" then waited for the response I always got.

"You are fo-ine. I thought you were a model or something. Do you have a wife?"

"Um, yes. I'm . . . Um, I'm married."

"You don't seem too sure of it. Is she making you happy?"

"Yes."

"You better be glad I like much-older men. Otherwise, I'd jump all over you."

"I'm sure they like you too," I said as I blushed.

"Do you?"

"Do I what?"

"Do you like me?"

"Yes. You're very nice."

"Thank you," she said as she licked her plump lips and leaned over to point at something on my computer.

Her breasts almost fell out of her blouse onto my desk, and her exotic perfume smelled heavenly. She had to know what she was doing to me. I turned the computer, so she could get a better view of the screen and hoped it would make her sit back in her chair. It worked.

"Thank you," she said.

"My pleasure," I sighed as I looked at all the activity going on in the office all of a sudden. I noticed most of the employees leaving, and I took a few shortcuts to speed up the process of her documents. I didn't want to end up alone with her sexy ass. I knew her type. She would be trying to lay me out if she found out the office was empty. I hadn't been getting any sex, so I didn't know if I could resist her if she tried. I imagined myself throwing all the stuff off my desk and bending her ass over it.

"All done. Anything else I can help you with?" I asked.

"My phone number is in my file." She winked. "Make sure you use it."

"It was nice meeting you, Tonette," I said, ignoring her flirtatious remark. *Maybe if I'd met you earlier, it would've been a love connection,* I thought.

I looked at the time on my cell phone. It was five fifty-five. I walked her to the door, watched her sashay out, locked up the office, and went to meet my brother.

Massey's was a bar we started going to when I was single. Known for its strong drinks and wild women, it was the place to be if you wanted to pick up a hot thing for the night. The place was full of bad-ass women who only wanted a night of unadulterated, kinky loving with no strings attached.

I arrived early, found two seats at the bar, and looked for my brother. Nolan was never on time, always claiming that the demands of the hospital held him up. Truth was, Nolan liked to be fashionably late so that he could steal all the attention, not that he needed to steal it. Women always flocked to him like bees to honey. He was in love with the limelight since birth and looked, acted, and dressed the part, just like our old man.

From what I could gather about our dad, he was a man who loved the ladies. He had women from all walks of life coming out of the woodwork, and he didn't discriminate. I heard we had black, damn near white, Asian, and Latino siblings. My mother used to say Nolan was just like him, but in actuality, I had some of his qualities too. We were blessed with his good looks but cursed with his high testosterone. I loved sex, wanted it all the time, and was lucky to find and marry a woman who matched my sex drive, even though she failed to do it recently.

Nolan and I didn't have any kids. I wanted some but hadn't been lucky enough to have any, Greg had one, and Nolan didn't want any at all. I figured he was either the luckiest man in the world, his pull-out game was fierce, or he invested in the best condoms money could buy. Either way, he dodged the bullet.

This bar was definitely not the place to be if you wanted to find a girl to bring home to mama. I surveyed the old and new faces, watching each one search for something to fill their needs when my eyes rested on Miko. She was wearing a tight white blouse, an even tighter red skirt, seven-inch red stiletto heels, red hoop earrings, bright red nail polish on her fingers and toes, ruby-red lipstick, and her face was beat to perfection. I had never fucked her, but I knew my brother had. The thought of touching her after him turned me off, and I scowled at her until she turned her head in shame.

"Hope you haven't been waiting long," Nolan huffed. He had on a navy dress shirt that showed off his broad chest, some blue Marc Jacobs slacks, and a pair of Stefano Bemer shoes. He was out of breath.

"Nope. I just got here," I lied. "You getting the usual?" I asked as I waved for the bartender to come over and take our order.

"Yes."

"What can I get you fellas?" she said, as she eyed us lustfully. We got that a lot.

"Gin and tonic for me and scotch and soda for my brother."

"So tell me, bruh, why are we here instead of in your game room watching me beat that ass in 2K14?" Nolan asked.

"I would *love* to see you beat my ass in anything."

"Tell me about this trouble in paradise."

"Darica wants a baby."

"Have you tried nutting inside her?"

"I've been doing that since we got married."

"You tried fucking her in all kinds of positions?"

"Yep."

"Massage therapy?"

"Yep."

"Did you go to a specialist?"

"We tried everything."

"Your wife seems like such a nurturer. I would never have thought she couldn't get pregnant," Nolan said as he sipped his scotch.

"*I'm* the one who can't get pregnant."

"What?" Nolan jerked and almost spilled his drink.

"I'm shooting blanks."

"Damn, bruh. Sorry to hear that."

"I've never felt so helpless in my life. I should've popped five babies in her by now."

"You guys could always adopt."

"I know."

"Or use a sperm donor."

"Word?"

"Sure. People do it all the time. You should visit that sperm bank on National Avenue. A few of my patients tried it, and they gave it a thumbs-up."

"That's not a bad idea, but I don't want some stranger knocking my wife up."

"They're not gonna fuck her, idiot. A doctor puts the sperm in her."

"I still don't want a stranger's fluids floating around inside my wife."

"Would you feel better if it were somebody you knew?"

"Maybe."

"I would volunteer my services, but your wife can't stand me. She would really hate my seed."

"She don't hate you. You're just not one of her favorite people."

"Shit, she hates my guts."

"If we need you, are you down?"

"Sure. Anything to help out the family."

"Thanks, man. Let me talk to her."

"Okay."

"Hey, man," I laughed and gestured toward Miko, "won't you call your girl over here for a drink, since she can't keep her eyes off of you?"

"That's all you, bruh," Nolan laughed. "Go on over there and give her the business, and while you're at it, take care of Big Booty Judy right there." Tonette was standing in the cut watching us.

"I have enough problems."

"I'll pass on that too, bruh," he said as Tonette winked and walked away, and Miko rolled her eyes at us and headed over to a group of soldiers.

Our half brother Greg walked in with his baby mama, Rella, on his arm. I shook my head. He had a beautiful wife at home, but there he was sporting this whore like she was a prize. She smiled and waved at us as they made their way over and ordered a few drinks. I didn't want them sitting by me because if Darica found out I was hanging with the enemy, she would throw my ass in the middle of next week. Greg's wife was one of her best friends.

"What's up, bro?" Greg bellowed as he gave me a pound.

"Not too much, man," I said. "What you got going?"

"Just trying to get out of the house for a bit. It's hot in there."

"I see. How's the wife?" I asked, not caring that I was pissing Rella off.

"She's good," he answered.

"I have to go to the ladies' room," Rella said as she stood up with a scowl on her face.

"Why you have to do her like that?" Greg asked after she walked away.

"It ain't like she don't know you married," I told him. "If you're unhappy with Chevette, you need to let her go on with her life."

"I love the hell out of my wife. I just need something more. You know how it is, don't you, man?"

"Nope."

"Look, I know I ain't no saint," Nolan interrupted. "But Chevette is a good woman. You better start watering that grass before it turns brown."

"I know what I'm doing. Y'all just jealous because I got two fine-ass women fighting over me. I can't help it if I got daddy's gift and use it to my advantage."

"I hope you wrap it up before you use it, or you'll truly get his gift of making babies. You already got one, and if one of those women decide to sleep around, you might catch something you can't get rid of."

"I'm all they need," he spat.

I guess that was his way of avoiding the issue. We spent the rest of the evening watching the crowd and making small talk as we finished our round of drinks. At a quarter past eleven, I gave my brothers a pound and left for the night.

I had about a twenty-minute drive home, and as soon as I got behind the wheel, my thoughts drifted on all the things my wife went through. She tried everything, from taking her basal temperature to pinpointing the days she ovulated. She douched with vinegar and baking soda, ate healthy foods, and went on bed rest. I fucked her from sunup to sundown, in the sixty-nine, wheelbarrow, and every Kama Sutra position known to man. But nothing worked.

The specialist ran all kinds of tests and found out that Darica could bear children, but my sperm count was too low to give her any. I felt like such a failure, and our world was turned upside down. She told me not to worry, that having children was not all that important, and I foolishly rationalized that it wasn't.

I was an insurance agent, so there were seldom reminders of what we were missing, but Darica was an elementary school teacher, and she was around children all the time. We had been married five beautiful years, owned a small home, and bought two cars. We managed to save $500 a month, which we used to take getaways during Darica's vacations from school. For two years straight, we took trips to keep our minds off having a baby. But, that changed the day of our flight from Florida to Los Angeles.

Our morning started out crazy. We woke up late, our taxi driver got lost twice and still demanded a tip, Darica forgot her favorite purse, and I didn't get my coffee before hitting the road. If that wasn't nerve-wrecking enough, a young woman got on the plane with a baby that cried the whole time.

Darica felt sorry for her because she spent most of the flight trying to calm her baby down. "She looks tired," Darica said. "I should offer to help so that she can get some rest. I bet I could get the baby to go to sleep."

"Go for it," I said.

"Forget it. God didn't give me children, so I guess I shouldn't meddle with anyone else's. I'm on my last chapter of this Carl Weber book, anyway," she said as she reached into her purse and pulled out her novel.

She was just about to read the last page when the pilot announced we were landing and thanked all the passengers.

"Are you almost ready?" I asked as we came to a safe stop on the runway.

"Yes. Let me grab my purse."

"OK."

"Excuse me," the young woman with the newborn baby called out to Darica.

"Yes?"

"Can you hold my daughter for a moment? I need to get a diaper out of our bag."

"Okay." Darica smiled as she took the baby out of the young woman's arms, cradled her tiny head, held her close, and inhaled the baby lotion on the child's skin. The infant nuzzled closer to Darica and took her finger into her tiny hand. Darica bounced the baby in her arms as other passengers skirted by them. Darica was in her own little world for about two minutes; then the young woman was done with her task.

"Ma'am?" the young woman asked. Darica ignored her as she sang a soft lullaby.

"Lady?" she asked firmly. Darica was oblivious to any outside noise as she hummed to the child.

"Can I have my baby back?" the young mother asked nervously.

"Huh?"

"My baby," said the now annoyed young woman.

"Oh. I'm sorry," Darica said.

The woman grabbed her baby and held her close as she quickly made her way out of the plane. She was so happy to have her child back that she forgot to thank Darica.

My heart went out to my wife. If I didn't know before, I definitely knew then; she was putting up a good act in front of me. She wanted children badly, and I would give anything I had to give her some. But I realized that was something that was just not in my power. I struggled to come up with an idea, but nothing came to me. Over the next couple of days, I watched her go from mildly sad to deeply depressed, and I felt helpless.

***

The sound of gunshots brought me back to the present, and I wanted to kick myself for taking the shortcut through the hood. It was the fastest route home, so I took it because I was so anxious to share what I learned with my wife.

Once I got out of harm's way, I started watching the kids on the block. Young girls not even old enough to understand life were pushing strollers with babies half of them didn't even ask for. Boys were hugging the blocks and slanging dope just to make ends meet. Some of them were barely out of diapers but had already fathered three or four children. I only wanted to give my wife one child. It was a damn shame that, out of all the people in the world, we were the ones deprived of something most people took for granted every day.

I started bobbing and weaving and had to roll down my car windows so I could stay focused until I pulled into my driveway. I staggered out of the car so smashed that I could barely walk and dropped my keys twice while trying to unlock the front door. On my third attempt, I was successful and even managed to make my way through the dark house.

I was excited to see my wife. She was lying in bed with the television on, not really watching the show. Her eyes were puffy from crying, her body was thin, and she was a shell of the woman she used to be, happy and carefree.

Usually, at this time of night, we would be noshing on high-calorie snacks and watching our favorite shows. Both of us had an excellent metabolism and never gained weight. But lately, she hadn't been in the mood to eat or do any of our favorite things. She had easily lost fifteen pounds, and her healthy butt and hips were nearly non-existent. Not only had she missed a lot of meals, but she had lost her desire for many things, including the most important, our sex life.

"Hey, 'Every Breath that I Take,'" I called out to her. It was my nickname for her.

"Hey, my 'First Love,'" she answered with mine.

"You busy?"

"No. What's up?"

"I want to talk to you about something."

"Okay."

"I think I have a solution to our problem."

"Dolan, I told you I'm over it. There's nothing we can do."

"Actually, there is."

She sat up in bed, looked at me with wide eyes, and gave me her full attention.

"What?"

"We should try artificial insemination," I said, standing back and looking at her as if I just came up with the most ingenious invention in the world. Darica stared at me unimpressed and answered unenthusiastically.

"I figured the last thing you wanted was another man's sperm in me, and I honestly don't think you can handle me carrying another man's seed."

"I want to do whatever it is that makes you happy."

"The question is, will *you* be happy?"

"If you're happy, I'm happy."

"Really?"

"Yes."

"Oh, baby. Thank you." Her face lit up with the first genuine smile she had in months. "I'll start making calls tomorrow. I love you," she said excitedly.

"I love you more."

Darica walked over to me, pushed me on the bed, kneeled in front of me, unzipped my pants, grabbed my rock-hard dick, and took it in her hot mouth. I moaned as she slid all of me inside it.

"Oooooooh, shit!" I yelled. I couldn't remember the last time I had a blow job, but I was pretty sure this was the best one I ever had. She was twisting my dick like a pepper grinder, using her saliva as lubrication, and moving up and down on me like she was obsessed. I hadn't had sex in so long that I felt like I was about to bust. I knew I needed to take matters into my own hands before I exploded in her mouth, and the whole thing would be over. It took some force, but I managed to pull my dick from her. Her suction was something serious. She had such a tight grip on me; it made a popping noise when it was released.

I ripped off her nightgown and exposed her beautiful body, sucked on her perfect breasts, and pushed two fingers into her wet tunnel at the same time. I licked her huge nipples and sucked like I was trying to get milk out of them. I brought my fingers to my lips and tasted her juices. She tasted so good; I headed south for more.

"Fuck me, Dolan," she begged, knowing if I started eating her now, it would be hours before she got this dick inside her. Darica loved my talented tongue action, but she loved getting fucked even more. I decided to give her what she wanted and slid my pole into her sopping wet pussy. I stopped when I saw I wasn't going to fit easily in her well lubricated but still tight opening and slowly started giving her every inch of me, while watching her moan in ecstasy.

"Ooooooh, baby. I forgot how good you feel."

"I'll never forget how good you feel. I love my pussy."

"Your pussy loves you too," Darica moaned as she tensed up and shuddered. "Baby, you're going to make me come."

"Come on," I demanded as I came deep inside my wife. She came before I even got the words out.

Chapter Three

Darica

We made love all night, overslept, and barely had enough time to shower. We ran out the door without breakfast, and as much as Dolan hated it, he had to start his day without coffee. He was nodding off as we waited to be called into the counseling office.

Dolan was a good husband who cooked, cleaned, and sent roses every week. He made it a point to take me to, or bring me, lunch at least once a month. He paid 75 percent of the bills, instead of splitting them fifty/fifty.

To top it off, he was fine as hell, with beautiful almond eyes, chiseled features that would give any male model a bad case of jealousy, and a body that could easily get him on the cover of the hottest men's magazine in the world.

He was also very sensual. I often came home to a lavender and rose bubble bath. He would wash me from head to toe, pat me dry, massage me with scented oils, and make love to me until I begged him to stop. I just wished all that bumping and grinding would have got us a baby to love. But that was one of those things that made a perfect marriage a nightmare.

I met him in 2009 at a club, of all places, that April had dragged me to. I didn't even want to go that night because she always disappeared shortly after we arrived. Her hot butt wasn't satisfied until she danced with every man in the place and got at least two or three phone numbers.

"Damn, he is fo-ine," she said as she waved to a tall, chocolate man with dreads. She licked her lips when she saw his dick print.

"Are you serious?" I asked.

"I don't know about you, but I came here to have a good time. Loosen your tight ass up."

"Here we go. I can't stand your ass sometimes. I could've stayed home and had a good time."

"Your ass always at home. That's why you don't have a man. I know your dried-up cooch ain't had none in a while."

"I'm supposed to get it here? No, thanks. You don't have a man either. Why do I have the feeling we'd still be here even if you did?"

"Yes, we would. I haven't met a man yet that can handle me. Girl, you better grab you one of these fine specimens. I know you want a little something-something in your life."

"I didn't come here for that, April. Your fast ass better be careful before you catch something you can't get rid of."

"I hope so," she said as the guy with dreads headed our way. He eyed her lustfully as she joined him on the dance floor. I shook my head, marched to the bar, and was standing all alone, minding my business when this tall, monster-looking fool approached me. Huge red zits studded his face.

"Hey, baby. Wanna dance?" he asked. I probably would have danced with him if he hadn't started groping me and pulling me toward the dance floor against my will. He was damn near dragging me across the room. My heels barely touched the floor as he pulled me like I had on skates.

No matter how hard I struggled, I couldn't get him to let go of my arm. Once we were in the middle of the dance floor, he held me against him and started grinding me as he pinched the hell out of my butt and forced his nasty tongue in my mouth. I was disgusted.

I tried to signal April, but she was too busy touching her toes with her eyes closed, while the man with dreads grinded up against her like he was having anal sex. As short as her skirt was, he might as well have ripped off her thong and stuck it in.

I managed to mush the monster's face with my right hand, pushed him off me with my left, and made a getaway. I was so focused on losing him that I ran clean out of the club, down the street, and into a dark alleyway. He was hot on my heels and grabbed me around my waist.

"You really fucked up brushing me off, bitch. I'm about to teach you a lesson," he threatened as he reached under my skirt, clawed at my panties, and hoisted my right leg up with his left arm. I looked up and saw a woman walking down the street.

"Heeeeelp me!" I screamed. She just rolled her eyes at me and kept on walking. I had pretty much given up hope when a man walked behind the monster and yanked him off me. I looked up and saw them fighting. The bastard wasn't so strong when he had to go neck and neck with a man. The man beat the shit out of the ugly bastard, then helped me up and halfway carried me back into the club. April looked frantic as he delivered me into her arms and walked away like nothing happened.

His woman looked angry; she had her hand on her hips, like she was going to knock him out. He looked like he was trying to reason with her that he was just doing a good deed, but she didn't care.

When I relayed the story to April, she apologized and said that she would never leave me alone again. I knew I had to find my rescuer and thank him, but he was nowhere to be found. I looked around for him as we exited the club and walked into the parking lot to get our car. I saw him as we were pulling off. He must have had a change of clothes somewhere because he was dressed in a different suit and didn't have a scratch on him.

"Thank you so much for what you did for me!" I yelled from the window.

"It was nothing," he said as he hunched his shoulders.

"That was really sweet of you."

"No problem," he said. "What's your name, beautiful?"

"Darica."

"Nice to meet you, Darica. My name is Dolan. I was wondering if I could take you out sometime."

"Sure." I smiled.

The next thing you know, I was marrying him. I walked down the aisle to our favorite song, "Endless Love" by Luther Vandross and Mariah Carey exactly one year later. That's how we ended up with the nicknames "First Love" and "Every Breath that I Take" or "Firsty" and "Every" for short.

Dolan's yawn startled me out of my blast from the past, and I nervously picked up every brochure in the place, searching for the answers to my questions about the procedure.

How much would it cost?

How long would it take?

What type of men donated sperm?

Would they exchange information?

Could they claim the baby as their own?

Will we have a multiple pregnancy?

How many tries would we get?

I was afraid to speak because I didn't want Dolan to change his mind. I was already worried that he was having second thoughts about being here.

"What made you think of this place?" I asked.

"Actually, I got the referral from Nolan."

"Your brother helped us?"

"He was the one that suggested it."

"Really?"

"Mr. and Mrs. Rogiers?" someone called.

We nodded our heads, nervously got up, and followed the counselor into the room.

"Hi, my name is Carlena, and I will be your counselor." Her eyes landed on Dolan's face, traveled down the length of his body, and back up again. She glared at him like he had just slapped her in the back of her neck, and I started to ask what the hell she was looking at. I knew my husband was fine, and women found it hard to control themselves around him. I decided to let her look, but if she got out of line, I was going to curse her ass out so badly, her boss would think her unprofessional ass committed a crime back here.

"Hello," we said in unison.

"Why are you here today?"

"We obviously want a baby," I blurted, like she just asked the stupidest question in the world.

"Have you thought about adoption?" *This smart-aleck heffa must be trying me,* I thought as I opened my mouth to say something sassy. Dolan beat me to it.

"Why would you ask us that?" he yelled. "If we wanted to do that, we'd be at an adoption agency."

"Calm down, Mr. Rogiers. I have to ask these questions."

Suddenly, I remembered that they do have a whole spiel they go through to see how serious couples were. I rubbed his arm to get him to calm down.

"Go on, please," I urged.

Carlena asked many more questions, so many that we didn't know what to think.

"Are you prepared to invest months into getting your child?"

"What do you mean months? How long is this going to take?" Dolan asked. He was obviously still on edge about the whole thing.

"I understand this is difficult, but I need you to keep an open mind."

"I'm so sorry," I whispered, then pleaded to Dolan with my eyes.

"Have you considered what type of father you're looking for?"

I swallowed a huge lump in my throat. We were not prepared for this line of questioning, and it felt more like we were in an interrogation room than a clinic.

"No," I stated. "What do you mean?"

"The race, height, weight, background, career, and education of the potential donor."

Carlena had succeeded in calming us down, and we gave each other a look of agreement that we would give in. We decided to give her a break and do our best to give her an idea of the man we wanted to bless us with a child.

"You did a wonderful job. I will contact you in a few days with a printout of the men that match your profile," she said. "You're in good hands with me. Don't worry, okay?"

"Okay," we said as she gave us the rate and payment plan information and thanked us before she politely escorted us out of her office.

As soon as I got in the car, I saw several texts from Chevette. Apparently, Greg had stayed out all night and came home smelling like another woman, whatever that smelled like. She suspected he was with his baby mama,

Rella, and threatened to put all his clothes outside. As much as I wanted her to do just that, I knew she wouldn't.

As a matter of fact, she was doing everything in her power to keep him when he obviously wanted the best of both worlds—his wife *and* baby mama. Chevette was trying to get pregnant when what she should have been doing was getting as far away from him as possible. If Rella's baby was his, he wasn't doing a damn thing for her, and it was pathetic. Chevette was the sweetest woman in the world, and she deserved better than Greg.

Me: Hold tight, girlfriend. I'll call you as soon as I get home.

Chevette: Thanks, girl. You are a true blue friend.

"What's wrong, baby?" Dolan asked me when he saw the expression on my face.

"It's Chevette. I wish Greg would do right by her. He came home smelling like some whore, and she's livid."

"That's too bad," he sighed. "Chevette's a good woman."

"I love my brother-in-law, but she's too good for his trifling ass," I said.

Dolan

I wasn't about to argue with Darica on that one, and I damn sure wasn't going to tell her I saw Greg with Rella. I knew that would start and all-out war, if not a string of questions, from what they were drinking to what kind of conversation they were having. Besides, I was pretty sure she got the picture when I said how good of a woman Chevette was and low-key implied that Greg was a dog.

I looked at my cell phone and saw that I had missed several calls from Nolan. I didn't answer the phone in front of Darica for obvious reasons, so I called him as soon as she walked into the kitchen to fix lunch.

He answered on the first ring. "Did you talk to her yet?" Nolan belted.

"Well, hey to you too, man."

"Sorry, bruh. I'm just anxious to see if she slapped you upside your head when you told her I was going to be the donor."

"I didn't exactly get to that part yet."

"How far *did* you get?"

"Well, I suggested we get artificially inseminated."

"And?"

"She loved the idea."

"So, what do I need to do now; go to the clinic and give them a sample?"

"Not yet."

"Did you tell her I was a potential donor?"

"I told her that it was your idea."

"That's it? What did she say about me?"

"She was impressed that you came up with it."

"But you didn't tell her I'm donating?"

"Not yet. I think it's best to get her used to the idea gradually. We did go to the clinic, met with a counselor, and got some info. She's looking through the brochures. They're gonna send us a list of potential donors."

"A list of donors on their list?"

"Yes."

"Damn, bruh. You know the best donor is me. I'm a blood relative. If you choose me, the kid will probably come out looking just like your nerdy ass. But it's cool. I respect your decision. I was only trying to help. If you don't need me, I understand."

"I see your point, but let me work on it. My wife needs to get used to the idea. Let her look at that list to give her something to compare to and *bam*—she's going to realize she needs you instead of those other guys."

"That sounds like a good idea, but how long do you think it's going to take?"

"Not long if you start coming over more, so she can get to know you and see how great you are. Let her see for herself that you're the best choice."

"You really think that'll work?"

"I know it will. From now on, I want you to come over on Wednesday and Friday nights."

"Friday?"

"Yes. Will that be a problem?"

"Friday is my date night. You know I have to keep my honeys happy."

"Can't you fuck your women on a different night?"

"Sure. I suppose I can change it to Saturday."

"Do you think you can tone it down a bit too?"

"What do you mean?"

"You have sex about four, maybe five times a week, right?"

"Well, yeah."

"How many times a session?"

"You starting to get personal, ain't you?"

"Just answer the damn question."

"I hit it about two or three times a night. Why?"

"That's too much."

"How do you know? You ain't no expert."

"How are you going to donate sperm if you don't have any?"

"I have plenty," he spat.

I was floored by the comment and was speechless for about ten seconds.

"I didn't mean it like that, bruh," he added.

"Come on, man. This is for the team. Giving up a few hours of pleasure will seem like nothing when you look into the eyes of your precious little niece or nephew."

"OK, bruh. I'm down."

"Oh . . . One more thing."

"Yes?"

"Make sure you wear a raincoat when you fuck those women."

"You ain't said nothing but a word, bruh. I got this."

"Thanks, man. I really appreciate it."

"No problem."

Nolan

I shook my head as I hung up the phone and went back to preparing my meal. My brother was a fool if he thought I was giving up my sex life. I wasn't about to take orders from him or anybody else. That fool had the nerve to tell me how to act. If I didn't know how to wrap it up by now, I was in serious trouble. My needs didn't disappear just because I was doing him a favor. As a matter of fact, one of those needs was about to knock on my door right now.

I warmed up the leftover chicken fettuccine on the stove, turned it on low, set the table for two, took out a bottle of wine, and put it on ice. I couldn't wait to get knee-deep in Evette. I hadn't seen her in a week and missed being inside her.

I took a quick look in the mirror when I heard the doorbell. I looked good, and I knew she was going to want to jump my bones. I was hoping to get some food and drink in me before we did it, though. I hadn't eaten all day worrying about Dolan's situation, so I was starving for food *and* love.

Damn, in a few months, I was going to have a junior or a little princess; something that would never happen if it was left up to me. I didn't think I could handle all the baby mama drama, responsibility, and child support. Lucky for me, it was a win-win situation. Here I was about to get a woman pregnant and still get to have fun and enjoy my life without baggage, while my brother took care of my seed and his wife got the bundle of joy she always dreamed about.

I smelled Evette's provocative perfume even before I opened the door. She had on her signature trench coat, and I knew that meant she had a surprise for me under it.

"Hey, E."

"Hey, Nolan. I was beginning to think you didn't want me anymore," she said as she batted her sexy, mascara-thick eyelashes. Her pouty lips begged for me to kiss them, but I knew if I did, it would be a wrap. "I haven't seen you in over a week. Have I lost my touch?"

"Never. Can I take your coat?"

"Not so fast, daddy. I smell that food cooking, and my mouth is watering. We better eat first because once I take this coat off, you will be eating me instead. I don't want to pass out on you."

"Suit yourself. No pun intended," I said reluctantly. "I'll feed you."

"I'm sure you will."

She grinned as she looked down at the bulge in my pants. Who was she trying to fool? Her ass wasn't going to faint. If it wasn't for that food, she would've attacked my zipper, pulled out my dick, and deep throated it right then and there.

She made her way to the kitchen table, sat down, and waited to be served.

My dick was so hard that I could barely walk. It was times like this I regretted the fact I was such a good cook. I hurriedly fixed the plates, threw them on the table, and shoveled my food down my throat. I watched as she devoured hers, ate a fair amount, and started to look like she was full; then, I made my way over to her side of the table and snatched her coat off.

"Goddamn!" I uttered. She had on a purple, lace panty bra set and stood up to model for me. Her ass and pussy print looked so good; I didn't know which one to devour first.

"You like?" she purred, knowing full well what her sexy ass was doing to me, and I was about to punish her for it.

"Hell, yeah."

I picked her up and carried her to my bedroom, where I damn near snatched the flimsy material off of her and dived into her wetness. We made love for hours, and it was half past eleven when we finally came up for air. I could tell she was a little upset when I pulled out of her right before I came.

"What's the problem? You have on a condom," she said.

"I just don't want any unwanted pregnancies."

"It's okay, baby. We've been together for a year."

"You know how I feel about babies, Evette."

"You don't have to take care of it. I'll do everything."

"We're not married."

"I would love to get married." She smiled as if I had actually popped the question.

I turned on the TV to change the subject. There was no way in hell I was having this conversation.

Darica

I had a migraine and didn't want to talk to anyone, but April had been calling all day, and I knew she was worried sick. We hadn't talked in over a week.

"Hey, bestie."

"Hey, bestie, my ass, bitch!" April yelled. "How come you haven't been answering my calls?"

"Sorry, *chica*. I've been busy."

"What the hell you been doing that you can't stop to call your best friend of ten years?"

"Me and Dolan are trying to get pregnant."

"So, what you're saying is you couldn't call me because he was knocking your back out? Nasty asses. Well, I hope it worked as long as you were gone."

"Stop being extra, April. Damn. It's only been a week."

"A lot happened in a week."

"Like?"

"Don't try to change the subject. I want to hear more about this baby. Do you want me to go get you a few home pregnancy tests?"

"No. It'll be awhile before you'll have to do that."

"Why?"

"We're having some technical difficulties."

"Say what now?"

"Dolan isn't producing enough sperm, and we have to get inseminated, and we're looking for the perfect donor, so we've been busy looking at profiles."

"Speak English, bitch."

I broke it down to April in simple terms, and she was silent on the phone for about six seconds.

"Are you there, chica?"

"Yes. I'm here, boo. I'm floored. I mean, damn; that's messed up. I'm sorry, sis."

"Me too. But I know it'll work out."

"You're better than me."

"Why?"

"If it was me, I'd be getting a divorce."

"What?"

"You keep saying *we* have to be inseminated, and *we* have to choose a donor. Dolan is the one who's shooting blanks."

"April!"

"There's no way in hell I'd take my hard-earned money and pay no sperm donor to fuck me when I could go to the club and get a man to do it the old-fashioned way."

"Your ass is silly, April. The sperm donor's not going to have sex with me. They're going to shoot the sperm in me."

"If I'm going to get sperm shot up in me, I'd rather do it the old-fashioned way."

"Girl, bye. You are nasty as hell."

"I'm keeping it real."

"Going to some nasty-ass club, picking up any old deadbeat nucca, and screwing him in the hopes of getting pregnant is stupid as hell."

"Well, try a college campus, then. The men are cleaner and smarter."

"April, you are all kinds of crazy, but I'm glad we talked about it. Now you can help me go through the profiles."

"How much will this cost anyway?"

"A couple thousand."

"Oh, hell no. I would be doing it the old-fashioned way and keeping my money in my pocket."

"You must be horny, the way you keep mentioning the 'old-fashioned way.'"

"As a matter of fact, I am."

"April, girl, I love you. But you ratchet as hell."

"I keeps it real."

"I need your support."

"Okay, girl. I got you. I'll be over later to help you look through that expensive-ass list of gigolos."

"Thanks. I love you."

"I love you more."

I hung up the phone, and it immediately rang again. It was my good friend, Nuni.

"What's good, girlfriend?" he blurted.

"Nothing much. How are you, love?"

"I've never been better. I'm feeling like you need to talk, and we are definitely past due."

"Yes, we are. You know me so well."

"What's the matter?"

I filled Nuni in on my present situation, and, as usual, he always tried to cheer me up.

"I would offer to help the cause, but my genes are so strong that the baby would probably come out acting just like my divalicious ass. But, at least she'll have a flair for fashion."

"I appreciate that, Nuni, but I think we got it under control. I just hope we can get the ball rolling soon. My biological clock is past due."

"I'm sure everything will work out. I gotta go. I love you."

"I love you more."

"Of course, you do."

Rolanda

Christmas Eve 1989

I was bent over the toilet vomiting up my breakfast when I heard someone knocking at the door. Since Mama wasn't home, I pulled myself up, walked over to the sink, rinsed my mouth out, splashed water on my face, patted it dry with a towel, and made my way down the hallway to the front door. When I opened it, I was horrified to see Brandon.

"What do you want?" I asked.

"I want my woman back."

"I don't want you."

"Can we let bygones be bygones, baby? I told you that wasn't my child."

"You never told me that. You said I don't work, and I don't pay for shit, and you can have whoever you want in your house. So, now you got it."

"Quit playing, Ro. You know I still love you, and deep down inside, you still love me too."

I swallowed the lump in my throat because Brandon was right. You didn't stop caring about someone just because they disappointed you, and you didn't stop loving them because they beat the shit out of you, either. I was young, but I knew what I wanted. It was Brandon.

He pushed me into the house, and the next thing you know, we were on my mother's couch making love like crazy. I knew it was wrong, so I said, "We have to get a room."

"Let's go back to my house."

"Isn't Landi there?"

"Hell no. I told you I didn't want her. All I want is my Ro."

Brandon opened the door for me, and I quickly walked out, closed it, and got in the car with him. He was speeding through Belle like he had a million dollars waiting for him, and when we reached our destination, thankfully without having a collision, he came to my side of the car, opened the door, yanked me out, and rushed me into the house. He had decorated it so beautifully that I felt like royalty. The Christmas tree in the living room was seven feet tall and adorned with beautiful bows and ornaments. There were five big boxes and two small ones under the tree.

Brandon took my hand and led me to the bedroom where we made love for the greater part of the morning and then fell asleep. When I woke up, the small gift I saw earlier was sitting on top of my stomach. I opened it, and there was a car key inside. I got up to look for Brandon and found him outside standing next to a blue BMW.

"Oh my God. Is this mine?" I squealed.

"Sure is."

"Thank you, baby."

I jumped into Brandon's arms and wrapped my legs around him. I was on cloud nine when I walked into our kitchen. I saw another small gift on the counter, so I opened it, and there was a house key inside. Suddenly, Brandon was behind me again.

"That's the key to our new house."

"You bought me a house too? How? When?"

"I got a promotion, and the first thing I wanted to do was share it with you and give you my name."

"Are you asking me to marry you, baby?" I said as I wrapped my arms around him and kissed him again. I almost wanted to call Mama. But I knew she wouldn't be happy about me being anywhere near Brandon after what happened on Thanksgiving.

I walked into the kitchen and busied myself, preparing Christmas dinner like I never left. I had just finished chopping my vegetables when I heard a knock at the door. Brandon was asleep, so I went to see who it was. When I opened it, I was surprised to see a woman with a 6-month-old baby in her arms.

"I don't mean no disrespect, but is Brandon here? This is his baby, and I heard he's denying it. I normally wouldn't do this, but I damn sure didn't want to call you, and I would never hurt another woman intentionally."

"Hold on," I said as I went to confront Brandon.

"Is there something you want to tell me?" I asked.

"What's wrong now?"

"There's a lady at the door holding a baby, and, from the looks of it, it's yours."

Without answering my question, he bolted out of his chair and ran to the door.

"What do you want, Eva?" he asked.

"I didn't make this baby by myself!" she yelled.

"How do I know it's mine?" he asked.

"I can't believe you would think it's not," she blurted.

"Get out of my face. Call me when you can prove it."

"I can't believe you, Brandon," she cried.

"I can't believe you're still standing here!" he yelled.

"Let's see how you feel when I file for child support," she warned him.

"Let's see how you feel when I throw you off my property," he said while wrapping his hands around her neck, causing her to gasp for air and almost drop her baby.

"Brandon," I screamed. "Stop!"

He let her go, and she walked away in humiliation.

"Sorry about that, baby," he said.

"Is it yours?"

"No. She's nothing but a ho. She doesn't know who she got pregnant by."

"What about Landi. Is her baby yours?"

"I doubt it. I haven't talked to her since Thanksgiving. Let's not argue about this, Ro. I know the baby you're carrying is mine, and that's all that matters," he said and walked into the bedroom as if nothing happened.

I walked in the kitchen, turned off the food, made a phone call, and sat in the living room. Ten minutes later, I walked out the door and shut it behind me. Before I could take my hand off the doorknob, Brandon yanked it open.

"Where the hell are you going?"

"Home."

"*This* is your home. We'll be moving into our new one this weekend, and we're about to set a wedding date, right?"

"No."

"What do you mean, no? We love each other, and you, me, and the boys are going to be a family."

"I don't want to be with someone that's abusive and doesn't take care of his responsibilities."

"I promised not to hit you anymore, and I'm trying to take care of you and my kids. I don't have any other priorities."

"What about the girl that just left here? She said it's your child."

"I don't give a fuck what she said."

"Exactly!" I yelled as I headed down the walkway.

"Ro!" he screamed. "Rolanda, get your ass back here. I'm not like your mother. If you walk away now, I won't be taking you back, and I'm damn sure not giving you that car."

I suddenly remembered I had the car key and reached in my purse, grabbed it, and threw it at him.

He looked hurt, then angry. He immediately ran toward me and balled up his fist. I closed my eyes and braced myself for the blow to my head when a car suddenly pulled up.

"Touch her, and you'll be picking your brains up off the sidewalk!" she yelled. It was Mama C, and, as usual, she was right on time.

"I'll see your ass again, Ro!" Brandon screamed as I ran to Mama C's car and got in.

Chapter Four

Nolan 2014

I completed the operation on my patient and looked at the clock on the hospital wall. I had an hour to spare and couldn't decide if I should go home to change and risk being late to Dolan's house or arrive early only to have to sit and wait for him.

By the time I left the hospital parking lot, I had decided to drive to their house, hoping someone was there to let me in. I knew if I called to let my brother know I was early, he would just tell me to use the emergency key. I always felt uncomfortable doing that, especially when the roommate didn't care for me.

The house was empty, and no cars were in the driveway. It was about eighty degrees outside, so sitting in the car wasn't an option. I reluctantly made the call to my brother.

"Hey, man," Dolan said.

"Hey, bruh. I got here a little early."

"No problem. The key is in the same spot. Just let yourself in. I'll let Darica know, and we'll see you in an hour."

"Cool."

I grabbed the key, unlocked the door, and walked into the house. Once inside, I realized how long it had been since I was last invited over.

The house looked like it was being renovated, and the changes they made so far looked amazing. Darica had definitely put a woman's touch on the place. She had the rooms fixed up so jazzy that I almost wished I had hired her to decorate my house. But I had a feeling that, even if it were her profession, she wouldn't waste her time helping me. There were pictures of them lining the walls of every room. They looked happy. They just needed a child to make their lives complete.

I grabbed a towel and washcloth out of the linen closet, went into the guest bathroom, and stopped clean in my tracks. There was an out of order sign over the tub. I shook my head. Only Darica would put a sign like this in a residential bathroom. I headed toward the master bedroom to take my shower.

Dolan

I called my wife five times, but she never picked up. I hated not being able to get in touch with her. "Hasn't her ass ever heard of an emergency? Is this how it's going to be when we have a baby?" I said while pushing the pound key. I waited for the beep and reluctantly left a message on her voicemail. At least this time, it wasn't full.

"Hey, 'Every,' I've been trying to get in touch with you. You need to start answering your phone. I could be hurt or something. Anyway, I'm calling to let you know that Nolan is going to stop by the house. Sorry for the short notice, but me and my brother need to bond. I told him to let himself in. I hope you don't mind. Make him feel at home, okay? I love you."

Darica

I had a major migraine, so I asked my assistant to finish my class. The pain was so excruciating that I barely made it to my car in the parking lot of Pine Elementary School, let alone the twenty-minute drive to my house. I managed to make it down the road without passing out and mustered up a small smile as I pulled into my garage.

I grabbed my purse and keys, ran into the kitchen, threw my clothes in the laundry room, and made my way to the bedroom. At this point, I hated that I had asked April to come over. The only thing I wanted to do right now was take a painkiller and sleep. I opened the bottle of pills, swallowed them, put on my sleep mask, and lay across my bed completely naked.

Nolan

I turned off the water, stepped out of the shower, and dried off my entire body before I realized I forgot my change of clothes in the living room. I walked out of the bathroom, slammed the door, and headed to get them. The sound of the door made Darica jump straight up.

"Aaaaaaaah!" she screamed. She didn't recognize me because she had on a sleep mask, so, in her mind, I was there to assault her.

I threw my hands up instinctively, and my towel fell on the floor. I grabbed her and put my hand over her mouth. She let out a muffled scream as she fought me. I slammed her into the bed facedown.

"Stop struggling," I said.

"Please don't do this. I'll give you whatever you want. Please don't hurt me," she pleaded.

I couldn't believe I was on top of my sister-in-law, and we were both completely naked. My dick was hard as a brick, and I wanted her so badly, it hurt. Everything inside me was saying "take her." My brother wouldn't be home for another forty-five minutes. I could do her and be halfway across town by the time Dolan arrived, and they would never know it was me. As if it was any justification, she hated my guts. I didn't care that she despised me. No matter how many women I had, I fantasized about my sexy sister-in-law on a regular basis.

While Darica's breathtaking beauty was one thing, sibling rivalry was another, and my brothers and I reached as far back as elementary school, and Mia, a girl I met on the first day of school in the third grade. She seemed to like me and spent a lot of time giving me ideas on how to finish our assignments. I, in turn, would give her my apples. I didn't like apples, and she couldn't get enough of them, but even if I loved them, when it came to me, she could have anything her little heart desired. I was determined to make her my girl, but she had other plans.

Dolan missed the first two days of school due to a cold but on day three, she saw his ass for the first time, and I became a distant memory. She ended up giving him her graham crackers and all of her attention.

"I don't like graham crackers anyway," she told him as she batted her long, beautiful eyelashes. Dolan ate that shit up. He gave her that crooked grin, said thank you, and proceeded to devour the snack as she watched him chew. The next thing I knew, they were the elementary school version of a hot item, declaring their love for each other and spending all their time together. They kicked me to the curb so fast that I was surprised they even remembered my name.

Maybe that was a silly reason to be angry at my brother, but I had no doubt I was harboring some type of resentment toward him for always being able to charm the pants off of women. He and I often clashed when it came to women, but I still didn't know if it was right for me to blame him for the attention I showered on his damn-near-perfect wife.

Outside noises snapped me out of my daydream and brought me back to reality. I knew I couldn't do this. She belonged to my brother, and this was not worth losing the relationship I had with him. The old-fashioned clock on the wall was literally ticking, and I knew what I had to do.

"When I take my hand off your mouth, don't scream," I whispered. She nodded her head in agreement. "This is not what you think. It's a misunderstanding. I was just using your shower. I would never hurt you. Do you understand?" She again nodded, though she had no clue who I was. She was terrified and wanted to do whatever it took to get me off of her. When I removed my hand, turned her over to face me, and took off her mask, she was in shock but definitely relieved as we stared at each other for a few seconds.

"Are we good?" I asked, my eyes pleading with her for understanding.

"Yes," she said, her eyes telling me she did.

I picked up my towel and wrapped it around my waist as Darica pulled the comforter over her naked body. She was trembling.

"I'm sorry for the misunderstanding. Dolan invited me over to . . . to . . . to . . ." I went completely blank. We didn't discuss what we would tell her. "He invited me over to hang out."

"He didn't tell me about it," she mumbled weakly. She was almost in tears.

"I'm sorry. He said he would call you. Check your phone. I'm going to get my clothes on," I told her. I ran out of the room, slamming the door behind me.

Darica

I locked my door, pulled the comforter around me, and cried like a baby. When I checked my phone, I saw that I

missed several calls and voice messages from Dolan. He
was always getting on me about answering my phone
calls and messages. I wanted to kick myself for not being
more obedient. All he wanted was for me to care about
my safety and well-being as much as he did. At that
moment, I wished I had listened to him more.

I tried my best to compose myself, but I was still
shaking. I'd just had the most terrifying experience of my
26-year-old life, only to find out that the brother-in-law
that I hated was my would-be assailant. I didn't know
whether to hug him or beat the shit out of him. All I knew
was, I was glad he wasn't a rapist.

For a fleeting moment, I thought he was going to
have his way with me. When he turned me over to face
him, he looked like he wanted to fuck me like there was
no tomorrow, and if he did, I probably wouldn't have
stopped him.

Standing at six foot two with rippling muscles and
washboard abs, Nolan was damn near perfect in his own
right. He was a little heavier than Dolan, his skin a shade
darker, and his hair color a sandier brown. I would be
lying if I said I didn't notice his slightly longer curved
member. I never thought about making love to another
man before today, and I struggled to keep the images
from flashing in my mind.

I definitely felt the chemistry between us, but I knew I
had to stop dwelling on it and get my act together. Dolan
would be home soon, and I didn't want him to see me like
this. It was enough that April's crazy ass was coming over,
and she would see right through me.

I stayed busy in the safety of my room because I didn't
want to risk having another awkward encounter with
Nolan. I changed the sheets and comforter because I was
certain my juices stained the bed and the scent of his
cologne was still there. I could still feel him, and I was
very confused about that.

He had stirred up something in me. My brain was on fire with the images of him and the way he handled me a few minutes ago. Once I got started, they would haunt me over and over until I felt crazy. I thought I had controlled them, but just like that, the flashbacks were back. For as long as I could remember, I'd had them. I didn't mind the good ones, but I definitely hated the bad ones.

Good flashbacks could be anything from remembering Momma pressing my hair and swearing up and down she didn't burn me, to helping Daddy mow the lawn. I wasn't much help because I was so little, but he made me feel like I was really doing something important. Afterward, Daddy would make the best barbecued ribs in the world, and Mama would whip up her famous potato salad and corn on the cob boiled in milk and sugar. Those were the times when we were a happy family . . . before she met Ben.

One night, Daddy and Mama had a big argument over something in the middle of the night, and by the time I woke up the next morning, Daddy was gone. To this day, Momma has never explained what went down.

She was an extremely beautiful woman, so I wasn't surprised when she brought Ben home. He had a nice smile, a handsome face, beautiful teeth, and was as tall as a tree. My mother loved Ben, though not as much as she had loved Daddy . . . until the day she found out he was a full-blown crackhead shortly after he moved in with us. I hated that about him. He tried to be as nice as he could, and on the days he wasn't using, he was a halfway decent guy. But he had a major drug habit, and when he was using, he was so ugly in spirit and angry; he hurt us to the core.

Sometimes, he would go a seemingly long time without using, and we would think he quit cold turkey. Then, out of the blue, he would go back on it again, hogging the bathroom while he hit his crack pipe and locking us out until we almost peed on ourselves waiting for him to come out. He stopped working—or rather lost his job—and he took money out of Mama's purse when she wasn't looking. She started stashing the money, but eventually, he became familiar with all of her hiding places.

"Hey, open up. It's me," April said as she assaulted my door. I scurried to open it as thoughts of Mama and Ben faded away.

"Hey, boo," I said as I pulled her in for a hug.

"Why you all cooped up in here with the door closed?"

"I was changing," I lied.

"Oh. So you couldn't let a bitch know that fine-ass nucca was here?"

"I'm sorry, love."

"He opened the door for me, and I was like, daaaaaamn. I wish I had worn my yellow dress."

"Not the yellow dress. You're trying to hurt the man?"

"If I get my hands on him, I'll tear him up."

"I'm scared of you."

"Dari, I know that's your husband's brother, but he is fine as a muthafucka. No offense, though."

"None taken. I don't blame you for looking. But you should reconsider trying to get at him. He has all kinds of hoes. The only thing he can offer is a hard dick."

"From what I can see, it is beautiful."

If only you knew, I thought as the image of it flashed in my head.

"I just need him for one night," she added.

"Nasty ass."

"Don't judge me."

"I'm just looking out for you, chica."

"I know. Are you ready to find these male prostitutes, I mean gigolos, I mean donors?"

"Yes. Let's head to the kitchen. I know you're hungry. I got some leftover lasagna from last night."

"Hell yeah. You know that's my favorite," April said.

I grabbed the sheets and comforter to throw in the wash on the way to the kitchen. I put the pasta in the microwave, April made a salad and heated some garlic bread, and we were ready to eat.

"Um, um, um. It smells good in here," Dolan said. Up to this moment, he and Nolan were in the den playing a game, and I hoped they would stay out of our way. I planned to call Dolan in to get their food so I wouldn't have to chance running into Nolan again. But Nolan was suddenly standing in the kitchen with us.

"Hey, my first love." I smiled as I kissed my husband. "How was your day?"

"Hey, 'Every.' It was okay. I tried to call, but you didn't pick up."

"I got your message at the last minute," I lied. "Sorry about that."

"It's cool."

"Hello, Nolan," I greeted him as if we didn't just have a close encounter.

"Good seeing you, Darica," he played it off.

"Nolan, you might as well sit down and eat with us," April blurted. I gave her the look of death, but she didn't notice. She was too busy looking at Nolan, who was watching me fix the plates. Her eyes focused on his lips, then down to his broad chest, and finally landed on the middle of his crotch.

"Thank you," he said as he gave her a knowing smile.

"So, Nolan," April pried, "I hear you're a surgeon."

"Yes," he answered.

"That must be a challenging job."

"Most definitely," he chuckled.

I couldn't stall any longer. I had to bring the plates to the table. Once I set them down, Nolan made eye contact with me and eyed me from head to toe. I knew he remembered me naked. He smiled and licked his lips. Everyone else was so busy eating that they didn't notice. I felt dirtier than I did when we were on my bed.

"So, how did you decide to become a surgeon?" April asked. I wanted to wring her neck.

"Well, actually, it chose me," Nolan told us.

"Nolan has always been the brains of the family," Dolan interjected.

"Yes. I have to admit, I was fascinated with dissecting insects and healing sick animals."

"Damn, really?" April gushed.

"He was carrying a 4.3 grade point average and was the valedictorian in high school," Dolan added.

"Aww, bruh, stop. You aren't so shabby yourself," Nolan stated. "You had a 3.5 GPA, and it would've been higher if you hadn't been focused on other things in high school."

"Like?" said April.

"Like girls," Dolan said.

"I was a late bloomer," Nolan explained.

"You didn't waste any time catching up," I snapped. I was silent up until now, and everyone at the table noticed my sarcastic remark. The image of Nolan's sexy body flashed in my brain. I couldn't focus, so I put my head down and ate my food.

The rest of the dinner was spent with Dolan trying to make Nolan look like some godlike Superman and himself only average. I couldn't understand my husband. It was like he was trying to auction Nolan off or something. When Nolan tried to imply that he wasn't all that, Dolan got mad at him. I was glad when they headed back to the den. April was so captivated by Nolan that she went in there with them. *Good riddance,* I said to myself as I sat alone at the table, pulled out my folder, and began to weed out the candidates.

"Sorry, chica," April said upon her return.

"I see you finally decided to let the boys bond."

"I can't help it. Nolan is fine, smart, talented, and successful. I have to have him."

"I told you, he's trouble."

"I'm sure if he finds the right woman, he'll be straight."

"You could care less about him finding Mrs. Right. You just want some dick."

"You don't understand. You already have a man, and I'm lonely."

"Nolan isn't man material."

"Speak for yourself. We have a date next week."

"Whatever."

"I like him," she said as she sat down and pointed to one of the men on my list to change the subject. By the time the night was over, we'd narrowed the list down to two.

Nolan

"Damn, man. I was trying to show Darica how great you are. You almost fucked it up!" Dolan complained.

"Shit, Dolan. You made me sound like a piece of meat. Won't you let me show her how great I am on my own?"

"We don't have that kind of time."

"I work fast."

"April came over to help her narrow down that list. I'm sure they nailed it by now."

"I got April under control."

"Fucking April is not going to get Darica to choose you."

"Who said anything about fucking her? I know how to sway a woman without pulling out my dick. Plus, I plan to go home with April to talk to her. I'll need two hours to do that; then I'll be back here to spend the night. I'll show Darica what a gentleman I can be. You just get your pitch ready. By tomorrow, she'll be begging me to be the donor."

"Okay, man. Do what you have to do," Dolan sighed.

"Thank you."

Darica watched as April and I drove away. April was as giddy as a schoolgirl, and Darica looked pissed that she allowed me to influence her so easily.

Once we arrived at April's house, I wasted no time grabbing her in my arms and holding her. April wanted me badly, and she thought I felt the same way about her, but, when she tried to kiss me, I turned my head, kissed her on the forehead and escorted her to the couch.

"I think you're a beautiful woman, but I have a lot on my mind. I only came here to get away from Dolan and Darica for a bit. I feel so helpless."

"Why?"

"Well, I heard about their situation, and I feel like I should be doing more."

"I know how you feel. I almost cried when Darica told me. But I'm sure they're grateful to have your support."

"You're right. I just wish that one of those guys on the list looked like Dolan and had the same upbringing. Shit, I'd be happy if they were from the same town like us."

"That would be nice."

"Yes. I want my brother to be able to look at the child and see himself."

"That would be nice. From what I looked at, none of the candidates are anything like him, and they definitely don't look like him."

"That's a shame. Well, at least they will have their baby. They're wonderful people. They will make great parents, no matter who they choose."

"It's too bad you can't be the donor."

"Me?"

"Yes. You're his brother, and you have the same DNA, the same parents, and the same background. That baby would be perfect."

"I never thought of that," I answered innocently, almost choking on my lie.

"You should offer."

"I'm sure Darica wouldn't want me. I'm not one of her favorite people."

"I could talk to her and make her see the light."

"You would do that?"

"Hell yeah. You're the perfect choice. Having you for a donor is almost the same thing as having Dolan."

"Damn, April. You're a genius. I'm excited I can finally help them."

Chapter Five

Dolan

I massaged Darica's feet and spent thirty minutes trying to convince her. When I was done talking, there was an uncomfortable silence. I took it upon myself to make the decision.

"So it's settled. When he gets back, I'll tell him he's the best man for the job."

"Not so fast," Darica whined. "There are two other candidates to consider."

"I thought you didn't want them. Every time I tried to get you to choose one, you had something negative to say about him."

"That doesn't mean I'm not considering them."

"I thought you wanted to do this as soon as possible. You said you were itching for it to happen."

"I want this more than anything in the world, Dolan. But I'm not about to make a rush decision on something this important."

"So, how long do you think you'll need?"

Darica looked at me like she wanted to slap the taste out of my mouth for being such an ass.

"Let me sleep on it," she told me.

I was pissed off because we'd been dealing with this situation forever, and even though I wasn't the one who had to carry the baby, I was her husband, and my feelings should've mattered to her.

"Take your time, baby," I said as I gave her a fake grin.

"Thank you," she whispered as I stormed off into the den and turned the volume up so loud, the sounds of 2K14 could be heard a block away. I glanced at her, and she looked at me like she would've thrown a brick at the game if she had one. Instead, she sighed deeply and went into our bedroom to get some peace before making the most crucial decision of her life.

Nolan

I arrived at Darica and Dolan's house exactly two hours later. I heard them arguing, so I stayed outside for ten minutes so they wouldn't be embarrassed; then I went to the guestroom, set my alarm for five in the morning, and lay down for some much-needed rest. When the alarm went off, I fixed eggs, bacon, crepes, and fruit for breakfast.

When breakfast was complete, I knocked on my brother's door and let him know I placed a tray of food out for them. I heard them thank me as I went down the hallway to finish painting a vase Darica had started, then headed to the yard to mow the lawn, do the landscaping, and trim the roses.

Darica must've devoured her breakfast, because the next thing I knew, she was dressed and admiring all the things I did for them. I was finishing up the yard when I noticed her staring at me. I wore a pair of shorts and no shirt. I had the body of a god. There wasn't a woman alive who didn't get horny from viewing it. I felt sorry for her when her guilty conscience got the best of her, and she looked around to see if her husband saw her watching me, then breathed a sigh of relief at not getting caught. Two seconds later, she was staring again. I just shook my head.

My brother tried to play it off like he and his wife were good. He even implied they had sex, but his body language told me different. Besides, I saw the den light on when I drove up last night, and that let me know he'd been in there playing the game since I left. He quickly retreated to their bedroom so I wouldn't know they'd argued. Maybe he sensed something in the air because he moped around the house looking for an excuse not to leave. I could tell he wanted me to finish my chores so that I could take my ass home. What man would be comfortable leaving his gorgeous wife alone with a brother whose body was a work of art, anyway? If it were my wife, I would've called off work.

After he left, I came into the kitchen for a glass of water. Darica was sitting at the table drinking orange juice.

"You're very talented," she said.

"How you figure that?"

"The breakfast, the vase, the landscaping, your profession, your smarts."

"Well, you have to eat, and this yard isn't going to take care of itself. My brother must be awfully busy with his job that he can't do those things."

"My husband gets pretty busy. He hardly has any time for . . ."

"For?"

"I don't think I should talk about that. Besides, it's not important."

"I'm sure everything you need is important. Come on. Let your brother-in-law in on it."

"I like to play Monopoly sometimes. But Dolan prefers 2K14. I also like to go out to eat, but my husband would rather eat at home. Personally, I think he wants to save money."

"I think you guys should go out sometimes. You know, splurge a bit."

"That would be nice."

"Where's that Monopoly game? I haven't played in years."

After I took my shower, I spent the morning playing Monopoly with Darica before asking her to get dressed up to go to lunch with me.

She came out in a tight, blue, minidress, her hair pulled into a messy bun, and shiny, red lips. She looked so beautiful that I wanted to grab her.

"You look nice," she said as she looked longingly at me. I couldn't say that I blamed her. I was clean shaven and had on a pair of slacks and a dress shirt that made me look sexy as hell. My expensive cologne was so intoxicating; no woman could resist it. I felt myself getting excited and grabbed my coat and keys to cover up.

"Thanks. Are you ready?"

"Yes."

I escorted her to the car and opened her door. As we sped through the city in my Ferrari, I realized we had never really talked this much in the years we'd known each other. Twenty minutes later, we pulled up to SeaBreeze, a fancy restaurant overlooking the ocean. The plates were very expensive.

We ate crab cake appetizers, lobster bisque, and a lobster shrimp medley for lunch, talked about everything under the sun, and found out we had a lot in common. Darica was stuffed. I wanted her to feel like she was being courted all over again, so I decided I wouldn't talk about the donors unless she brought it up. April was scheduled to call her about it at three anyway.

"Nolan?" a voice from behind me sang. I winced as I turned around to hug the woman standing there.

"Hello, beautiful," I said.

"So, this is where I have to go to find you," she pouted.

"You make me sound like a stranger."

"I haven't seen you, and you've been so distant that, even when I do talk to you, it's like I'm talking to somebody I don't know. I'm beginning to think Dolan is the only son I have."

"I'm sorry, Mom. I'll do better." I cringed at the comparison.

"Hello, Darica," she said as she embraced her daughter-in-law. "Do I have any grandbabies on the way yet?"

"Not yet, but we're working on it," Darica smiled.

"I can't wait. It doesn't look like Nolan is rushing to the altar, so you and Dolan are my only hope."

"Um, Mom . . . You're looking lovely."

"Thank you, son. I just got my hair done."

Darica patted the silky curls on her shoulder. "You do look gorgeous," she added.

"So do you, love. I see I need to talk to Dolan about taking you out, instead of asking his brother to do it."

"Darica happened to run into me here on her lunch break," I lied. "Dolan takes his wife out all the time. He doesn't need to be scolded about it," I said as I looked at my mother, as if to warn her not to say anything to him.

"Well, enjoy your lunch," she said.

After she walked away, I asked for the bill, suddenly feeling uncomfortable about being out with Darica. I paid it, escorted Darica to the car, and sped to her house in ten minutes, hoping I had worked enough magic to get on her good side.

When I pulled up in front of the house, I noticed she was a little sad. I hoped it was because she didn't want our "date" to end. I walked her to the door, and her phone started ringing.

"It's April. I better answer," she whispered. "Thanks for a lovely day."

Right on time, I thought. "You're welcome, love," I said as I handed her a $200 gift card from the restaurant and hugged her. "Let's keep this a secret, okay? No one needs to know I took you to SeaBreeze."

"Of course," she said as I walked away, and she took her call.

Darica

"Girl, I've been blowing your phone up. Where have you been?" was the first thing I heard April say.

"Sorry, April. I was hungry. I went to grab something to eat."

"You better slow down. You're going to be having a baby soon, and you don't want to gain too much weight before you conceive. I'm not lifting your fat ass out of the tub or nothing."

"Yeah, right. What's the urgency, chica?"

"Nothing. I was just wondering if you made a choice yet. I didn't like any of the candidates."

"I thought you said you loved the two we picked out."

"I think we need to go back to the drawing board. None of them look like Dolan, and they have nothing in common with you or your husband."

"I'm not picking that Ukrainian guy."

"Nobody said anything about him."

"You think we should keep looking? I was hoping to nail this soon."

"Well, I think we should start interviewing people in his family. Does he have any cousins or a best friend?"

"The only suitable family member I know about is his brother, Nolan. I'm not even thinking about Greg's crazy ass, and most of his cousins are female. The rest live out of state."

"Do you think Nolan would do it?"

"I don't know."

"Oh, I'm sorry, girl. How insensitive of me. I know you hate his guts."

"I don't hate him. I think he's cool."

"Since when?"

"Since I got to know him better. He's grown on me the past few days. He's smart, talented, handsome, and healthy; not to mention he looks like Dolan and came from the same family. The baby would practically look just like Dolan's twin."

"So, all we have to do now is tell Dolan you made your choice. Nolan's your baby's father."

"I don't know. I just had a big argument with Dolan over him mentioning it the other night."

"So, he's on board with it too?"

"Yes."

"It's settled then."

"Nolan is a single man. He might want to have kids of his own someday."

"Somehow, he doesn't strike me as the fatherly type."

"I don't think we should burden him with this."

"He should be happy to do this favor for you. Besides, he won't be the one carrying the child. We just need his sperm. He won't even have to take care of it. How cool is that?"

"I guess you're right. But for all we know, he might think it's a terrible idea."

"There's only one way to find out."

"Okay. You win. I'll talk to my husband about it."

"Yaaaaaay!" April screamed. "You're going to be a mother. I'm so happy for you."

"So am I."

After I got off the phone with April, I fixed dinner and dessert and waited until Dolan was full. He overate as usual and was nodding off at the table when I nudged him. "Baby, can we talk?"

"Sure. What's on your mind?"

"I've made a decision."

"You did? About what?"

"I want Nolan to be the donor."

"Wait. What?" He straightened up in his chair and rubbed his eyes to make sure he wasn't dreaming.

"I think we should ask Nolan to be our baby's father."

"That's what's up. I'll let him know. I'm excited that we're keeping it in the family. Now I really feel like I'm about to be a daddy."

"I really feel like I'm going to be a mother."

"OK. Let me contact Nolan."

Dolan

I was happy on the one hand, but on the other, I was horrified. I always thought I would father my own children or have none at all. Now that Nolan was going to be the donor, I was a little afraid that our lives would change.

I didn't know if I could look at his child, knowing that when it called me daddy, I would not truly be. My brother was about to be the true father, and that made me feel some type of way. I wondered if I could resist the urge to think of Nolan as the father, or would I automatically think of myself as the child's father? And how would I, in all honesty, refer to Nolan as uncle when I knew it was truly Nolan's blood that ran through the child's veins?

What if Nolan tripped out and wanted to claim the child as his own? Would we have a legal battle on our hands? Would we have to confess this to the child? It was so nerve-wrecking that now I wished I didn't have to tell Nolan right away. But we had made it to this point and had to move forward.

It was five o'clock in the evening, and I turned in early after powering off my cell phone, so I wouldn't have to face the many calls Nolan placed to me. Nolan was no doubt anxious to hear the news, but he would have to wait while I slept on it. I would call him in the morning and get the ball rolling.

Nolan

I stared at my cell phone for the twentieth time with a confused look on my face. All of my calls to Dolan were going to voicemail. I wondered if something happened or if my brother had changed his mind about using me as the donor. It had to be hard on the man, not being able to impregnate his wife and having to rely on his brother to do the job. But they wanted a child, and it was what it was. However difficult it might be, it was the only way they would be parents. Eventually, we would cross that road, and soon things would be back to normal.

I couldn't wait to see my seed. I always wondered what a little me would look like, but I honestly thought I would never get a chance to witness it because, let's face it, I'd never been the marrying type. Only once did I consider getting married, and I sure as hell wasn't the type to allow a woman to use a child to control me. That would probably be the only child I would ever have since I didn't plan to ever have a baby with a woman on my own. I was excited about being able to admire and hold this child with no strings attached.

They had to know I was anxious to hear what their final decision was, whether they chose one of the clinic's donors or me so that I could get on with my life. Either way, I would be cool.

Rolanda

1990

It was hot as hell outside, and I still hadn't gotten a car. But I did manage to find a job at a local restaurant that was only one bus ride away from home. I felt lucky to have it because I had two sons to take care of.

Brandon wasn't helping with any money for our 6-month- and 1-year-old boys, and if I mentioned child support, he threatened to beat the shit out of me. I had pretty much given up on him, especially since every time he thought about it, he was knocking on our door asking me to make love to him or come back home. Mama would scare him away with a gun or the promise of a beat down from one of my cousins, and he would leave, vowing to get back at us.

The restaurant I worked at, Borderline, was busy, especially at lunchtime. I wasn't feeling all that well, had gotten very little sleep, and was cranky today when *he* walked in.

That man had to know how fine he was and how badly I wanted him. He had the most beautiful bone structure and the prettiest eyes I'd ever seen on a man. Every time he came into the restaurant, he was always cleanly shaven with a fresh suit and colorful tie. He had on a neon green one today.

Why he took time out of his busy schedule to stop in, I would never know. What I did know was, anything he wanted, I was breaking my neck to give it to him.

"Go on over there," my coworker, Millie, said. "You know you want to."

"That's not my station; it's yours," I said.

"I can't be his waitress right now. I'm on my break," she replied as she popped her gum and walked away like I wasn't there. I swallowed the lump in my throat and walked over to him.

"What can I get you today, sir?"

"I'll take a cup of coffee and your phone number," he smiled. I smiled back and went to put in his order. When I returned he asked, "Can you sit down and talk to me for a minute?"

He would have to ask me now.

"You trying to get me fired?"

"No. I just want to get to know you better. You are beautiful."

So are you, I almost said out loud. "Thank you, sir, but I have to go."

"Wait," he said as he grabbed my arm, sending electric currents through my body. "When is your lunch break?"

"In about fifteen minutes, so, if you don't mind, I'd like to get you your coffee so I can head out."

"Can I take you to lunch?"

"My break is only thirty minutes. By the time we get to the restaurant and eat, it'll already be over, and I'll be in trouble."

"Well, can we eat here?"

"I don't eat here."

"Why?" he asked curiously.

"Because I don't like the way they prepare the food."

"Really?" he said. "What else don't you like about this place?"

"The decór, the tables, the atmosphere. Oh, and the prices are ridiculous."

"Damn, beautiful. You really laid it out, didn't you?"

"Well, you wanted the truth, right?"

"Yes, I did."

"I don't think it's a good idea to date the customers anyway, so if you will excuse me, I'll go get your coffee and be on my way."

"But I'm not a—"

I walked away before he could say anything else, and I felt kind of sad about it. But I realized I couldn't blame anyone but my dumb ass because I was being so silly. I said all the wrong things.

"Damn, girl, I think he likes you," Millie said.

"I like him too, but I think I blew it."

"How?"

"I turned down his offer for a lunch date."

"He would have had my ass."

"There was no way I could've gone out with him and got back in time without losing my job."

"He would've helped you."

"How?"

"You don't know who he is?" Millie laughed.

"He's just some random customer, right?"

"He's the owner, honey. His name is Phillip."

"Shit. I *double* blew it. After what I said about this place, he's going to fire me for sure."

"If all you can worry about is losing your job, you're really twisted."

I ignored her, ran to my locker to grab my purse, and hoped he wouldn't see me as I slipped out the back. As I made my way down the street, I noticed somebody in a blue Toyota with tinted windows following me. I turned to run and found myself in an alley. I ran as fast as I could, scared out of my wits and afraid to look back, knowing whoever it was, was going to hurt me. He parked his car, got out, and started running after me. It didn't take him long to catch up with me, and he grabbed me and spun me around.

"I told you I was going to catch you by yourself," Brandon smirked.

"What do you want?"

"You."

"Why would I want somebody who don't even help take care of his sons?"

"You can have all that if you move back in with me."

"I don't want you anymore, Brandon. I can make it on my own."

"Get your dumb ass in this car. You can't take care of our kids. You're over here waiting tables."

"I'd rather die than be with you."

"Don't tempt me. I've been watching you. I could've killed you if I wanted to."

"Do what you have to do even if it means I have to leave this alley in a body bag!" I was screaming when we heard footsteps approach us and a man speak.

"I don't think I heard you right," Mr. Neon said to Brandon. "Are you threatening this woman?"

"Man, this is between me and her. It's none of your business."

"Is this what you want, Rolanda?" Mr. Neon asked.

"Hell no."

Brandon grabbed me from behind and put a knife up to my neck. I immediately felt bad because I knew Brandon would slit my throat and end my life, and I felt guilty because I brought an innocent person into this mess.

"Just walk away, man," Brandon warned him.

A Lincoln Town Car came down the alley and out jumped two seven-foot men. Brandon looked like he was going to piss in his pants.

"I'll see you around, Ro," Brandon said as he ran down the alley.

"Thank you," I said to Mr. Neon. My hands were still trembling as he escorted me into the car.

"You're welcome, beautiful. Where to for lunch?"

It turned out that Mr. Neon, also known as Phillip Rogiers, owned five Borderline Restaurants, two fitness clubs, eight grocery stores, and a car dealership. That lunch turned into several dinners and me leaving my job at the restaurant. I became his business consultant after the advice I gave him about Borderline. He changed the décor, the way the food was prepared, and low-ered the prices. He called me his lucky charm.

We got married, and he adopted my two sons, Dolan and Nolan, as well as Landi's son, Greg, after she had a nervous breakdown. I guess Mama was right. Running wasn't always the smartest thing to do. There was always a better way to deal with things.

Chapter Six

Darica 2014

I woke up bright and early and looked at my sleeping husband. He went to bed early and was apparently still tired. He had gone through a lot while I made my decision, and I knew he was somewhat relieved that I made a choice, but I hoped he was as ecstatic as I was. I couldn't wait for him to wake up, so he could call Nolan and find out if he still intended to help us out, and if so, find out when he wanted to start the process.

The counselor told us that it could be as quick as getting pregnant on the first try or months of agonizing treatments and inseminations. I hoped to get pregnant right away. My biological clock was past due, and I was anxious to experience motherhood and all the perks that went along with it.

Nolan

I walked out to my car three times to go to Dolan's house, but each time, I felt stupid and returned to my house to wait for his call. I didn't want to seem overly anxious, but I didn't think it was fair of them to ask for my help, then leave me hanging. This was starting to take control of everything in my life. I couldn't eat, sleep, or work from worrying about their decision, and I was mad as hell.

"Are you all right, Doctor?" the nurse asked.

"Yes. Why?"

"You're just staring into space. We need to get this patient prepped so you can operate."

"I'm sorry. I'm not feeling well today. I think I need to call in another surgeon."

"There's no time for that. We need to do something about this wound right now."

"You're right," I said as I lined up my instruments and began working my magic on my patient.

I was livid, but I still managed to make the right incisions and save my patient's life. I was, no doubt, a professional, and in thirty minutes flat, I had her stabilized and ready for recovery. I washed up and went out to tell her family she was going to be okay.

"Thanks, Doc. You're a miracle worker," the woman's husband praised me.

"It's my honor," I smiled. But I felt ashamed for allowing something so trivial to get in the way of saving someone's life.

Dolan was not only ignoring me, but he also had turned off his phone completely. I knew he was having second thoughts about using me as the donor. He knew the minute Darica got pregnant that their lives would change. She would focus on prenatal care, food cravings, maternity clothes, formula, Lamaze classes, the nursery, baby showers, and her baby daddy. Dolan would never be able to handle the fact Darica had my seed growing inside her and not his.

All this talk about wanting me was just a game that Dolan never thought would actually come to pass. Now that it had, he wanted to backtrack. But it was too late.

His wife would make his ass miserable until she got her baby. He would have to call me eventually.

Dolan

I ate my breakfast, got dressed, and made my way to work. I was mad at myself for not being able to make that phone call to Nolan. I realized how selfish I was for holding up progress. After all, it was my idea to suggest a donor, when Darica would have been just as happy with adoption. Now, I had to do something or watch my wife go into a deep depression again.

I thought about going to another specialist to see if they could test me again, give me a pill to increase production of my sperm, or see if they could do something to extract it from deep within my body. But that would require more time, something I didn't have.

I knew I was fighting a losing battle. This was the only way I could give my wife the child she so desperately wanted. It was a blessing I even had a brother. Now, there would be no question that the child was a member of our family. I said a silent prayer that, in the end, Nolan and Darica would brainwash themselves enough to see me as the father as I picked up my phone to call Nolan.

Nolan

"Hey, bruh!" I yelled into the phone. It took everything in me not to curse his ass out for keeping me in suspense.

"Hey, man. Sorry I didn't call sooner. Been busy trying to convince Darica."

I felt like he was lying. "So, what's the verdict?"

"She wants you to be the donor."

"Really?"

"Yes."

"That's what's up. Congratulations. You're going to be a daddy."

"Thanks, man. Can you come over tonight so that we can discuss the details?"

"Sure."

Darica

I was excited and nervous that Nolan was coming over. I hadn't seen him since we spent the day together, and I had mixed emotions. I tried on three outfits, none of which seemed right for the occasion. I knew it was silly, but I wanted to impress him. I finally settled on a basic blue jumpsuit and wedges.

Nolan arrived promptly at seven p.m. making a T-shirt, Seven jeans, and a pair of Jordan's look sexy. His Gucci cologne had my heart racing, and I had to compose myself before talking to him.

"Thank you for what you're doing for us," I said.

"It's my pleasure. The look on your face is thanks enough," he said as he gave me the once-over. I noticed his flirtatious look and hated myself because I loved how it made me feel warm all over. I wished I could turn back the hands of time and go back to hating him.

By the end of the evening, we had mapped out a plan that worked for all of us, and I was glad when he left. My nerves were bad. I just wanted to turn in early. As soon as I got my nightgown on, April called.

"Girlz nite alert!" she shouted.

"Well, hello to you too, sis."

"Sorry, Dar, but we have a crisis here, and we need to have a girlz nite as soon as possible."

"No problem. What's up?"

"It's Chevette. She's depressed. Says she's thinking about doing something crazy."

"Crazy like what? Killing herself?"

"No. She's not that crazy."

"Okay. Well, set it up. I'll be ready within the next hour."

By the time the ladies got to my house, Chevette was a complete and total mess. She had apparently argued with Greg, and she wanted to vent. Greg had been out all night with some woman, most likely his baby mama, Rella, and Chevette was tired of the drama.

"So why don't you leave that fool?" April said as she handed Chevette a Tequila Sunrise.

"And do what?" Chevette asked. "Go out and find someone else?"

"That's not a bad idea," April said. "They say the best way to get over one man is to get under another."

"I think she needs to go find some peace of mind," I said.

"Greg is all I know. I don't even know how to act around anybody else, and I don't know how to be by myself."

"So, you'd rather stay with him and let him fuck Rella?" April blurted.

"No, I don't want that either."

"You are too beautiful to be sitting around waiting for Greg to act right. He's never going to be anything more than what he already is—a player," April told her as she picked up her drink.

"We're almost in our thirties. I think he'll settle down soon," Chevette said as she took a sip of hers.

"You think he's going to settle down with you or one of the other bitches he's been fucking?" April asked. I looked over at her like she was crazy.

"What?" she said. "I'm just keeping it real. She needs to leave his ass while she's still young and attractive. There's good men out there. I may not have one, but I'm working on it, and I damn sure ain't waiting around for no loser to stop fucking other bitches. It's just nasty."

"I hear what you guys are saying, but it's not that easy. I love him."

"Then I guess you're going to love everything he does to you," I said.

"What she needs to do," April said, "is get her a new and improved man. I believe in that shit," April scolded. "She needs to kick Greg's ass to the curb and show him what she's made of because, apparently, he does *not* know."

"I think he's just acting out," Chevette countered.

"How you figure that?" April asked.

"I know he's upset because I haven't gotten pregnant yet," she explained.

"If you stop letting that fool drive you crazy, you probably would've been pregnant by now," April advised her.

"Maybe you need to be pregnant by another man, someone who can treat you right during your pregnancy," I said.

Chevette didn't appear to be considering any of our advice at all. I had to wonder why she even wanted to have a girlz nite. What did she think we would say? Stay with him and work it out? Maybe she thought we would whoop his ass and make him do a one-eighty. The truth of the matter was there was nothing anyone could do to help her. "You are the master of your fate and the captain of your soul," I told her.

"Amen to that," April agreed.

We took several more shots of Tequila and fell asleep in the den. Chevette slept like a baby, probably for the first time in a long time. I wasn't about to wake her up and interrupt her peace. "Sweet dreams, my loves," I said as I covered her and April with a blanket.

At around three in the morning, Greg came knocking on my door. "Chevette here?" he asked. I made his ass wait outside while I woke her up and asked her if she wanted to see him. Of course, she said yes and almost broke her neck putting her shoes on. That almost made me wish that I had told him she wasn't here. Let him squirm a little bit.

Chevette didn't realize it now, but she definitely had the upper hand. All she had to do was do a disappearing act, refuse to see him, and go on a few dates with other men, even if she wasn't feeling them, and he would be straight. It probably wouldn't stop his cheating, but it would make him feel uncomfortable, which was exactly what he needed. I could see in his eyes that he loved her, but he had no respect for her, which meant he would do whatever he wanted to do until she put her foot down. One day she would realize that, but it wouldn't be today.

Chevette quickly put on her coat and thanked and hugged me so she could jump into Greg's arms. I shook my head. If she liked it, I loved it.

Rolanda

1991

I couldn't believe my eyes when I stepped out of the limo and saw Landi. When she came to my house that dreaded Thanksgiving Day, she was a halfway decent-looking chick, but looking at her right now was an entirely different story. She had on some tattered jeans and a faded out blouse, and I was not talking about in a tie-dye, good way. It was fucked up.

She was pushing her baby in a beat-up old stroller, and he looked like he hadn't had a meal in days. I thought that the next time I saw her, I would smirk at her as I sashayed by in my designer clothes, and she would be dripping with jealousy.

But, surprisingly, I felt sorry for her and even more so for her child. I wondered if the baby was Brandon's, as I calculated a quick timeline in my head. If it was his baby, I could understand why it wasn't being taken care of.

"Are you okay?" I asked, wondering if she recognized me. I was dressed to the nines in Gucci from head to toe, my hair in a beautiful updo, a huge diamond rock on my hand, and my limousine driver by my side.

"Hell no!" she screamed. "That low-life son of a bitch Brandon hasn't helped with his son, he won't give me money, and we haven't eaten in days."

"Is there anything I can do for you?" I asked her. After all, I felt somewhat responsible for their demise.

"We just need some food. Then I'll be strong enough to take care of my son."

"No problem." I motioned for her to get into the limo.

"Damn. This is a nice come-up," she said.

"Yeah. A far cry from what Brandon was offering."

"Amen to that." She nodded. "At least one of us got lucky."

I realized I could have dropped her off at some diner, gave her a twenty-dollar bill, and sent them on their way. But I felt sorry for them, and part of me wanted my sons to meet their brother. I took them to my house, escorted them into the kitchen, and the next thing you know, Landi and I were talking like old school pals.

When evening came, I took them both into a guest room and went to bed. When I woke up, she was gone, but Greg was still there with a note attached to him. It said:

Please take care of my son. I know I seem like a deadbeat mom, but I really want to be able to care for my child. It's just that, in the predicament I'm in, I'm not fully able to. But in a few months, I will be. I'll come and check on him next week.
Love,
Landi

Landi kept her word and checked on Greg every week. But the downside of what she called her *predicament* was she was addicted to crack so badly, that sometimes, she was incoherent. I had the guards watch my house to make sure she didn't steal anything, and I always kept her fed. The next thing you knew, she had had a nervous breakdown and was institutionalized. I raised Greg as my own son.

Chapter Seven

Nolan 2014

After two months of questionnaires, STD tests, counseling sessions, prying into my personal business, and abstaining from regular sex just so I could ejaculate into a cup every three days, I was getting fed up. Darica was nowhere near pregnant, and I was beginning to feel played.

I had completely stopped having sex with Evette, and she thought I was crazy because she was throwing herself at me every chance she got, and I refused to take it. She showed up unannounced a few times, and I cursed her out. She was thoroughly convinced that either I was pussy whipped from another woman or gay.

Dolan and Darica had blown through their savings—and some of mine and April's. They only had enough money for a few more treatments before they had to give up until they acquired more funds. Even with medical insurance and the loans they took out, it was getting tight.

It was a cold day in November, and we were discussing our options. We knew our parents had more than enough money to help, but that was the last thing we wanted.

"Thanks for trying to help us, man. I'm sorry we dragged you through this, but we're going to have to stop the treatments for a while. I'll try to pay you back a couple of thousand in a few months," Dolan said.

"Don't worry about it, man. You all have been through enough," I said.

"A couple of thousand?" April blurted. "Damn. I think that clinic is taking you all for a ride. For that much money, you may as well do it the old-fashioned way."

April had been drinking like a fish and running off at the mouth since she arrived. Most of the time, we didn't take anything she said seriously, but this time, she was on to something.

"April," Darica said sternly.

"What you snapping at me for? You know I'm right. He can get you pregnant in a heartbeat if you have sex with him. Shit, it ain't nothing but a business transaction. You don't want him anyway. You love your husband."

"I'm sorry, guys," Darica apologized. "I think she's had too much to drink."

"I think she has a point," Dolan sighed. "It's just business, right?"

"Thank you, Dolan," April said. She was relieved that someone liked her idea. "See, Darica? Even your husband agrees with me," she slurred. "Don't worry about it. Nolan's fine ass can fuck me and nut in you if necessary, but this shit is for the birds. You all have been at it much too long, and it's getting outrageous."

"I don't think we'll have to go that far, April," I said. "I can pleasure myself and enter her at the last minute. I'll barely have to touch her, and she'll probably get pregnant faster that way than anything."

"Don't douse my hopes, Nolan!" April yelled.

"I don't know if I can do it," Darica protested.

"It might not be that bad, baby," Dolan told her.

"Who are you to say it's not that bad? *I'm* the one who has to spread her legs and commit adultery. I didn't get married to step out on my husband," Darica snapped.

"Whoa, baby. Calm down. Everyone's just trying to help. We didn't mean to upset you," Dolan whispered.

"If you want to help, think of a way to get more money so we can continue those treatments!" she yelled as she walked out the door, slamming it so hard, the windows shook.

Darica jumped in her car and sped off so fast that we smelled rubber. Dolan and April were blowing up her phone, but she wasn't thinking about answering it. We felt bad for her. She had no one else to talk to about this and not too many options.

Dolan

I walked through the empty house in one of the most fucked-up moods I had in a long time. Food cartons, soda cans, and plastic forks that should've been thrown away days ago were strewn about. The bedroom hadn't been cleaned in days, and the bathroom smelled awful, but I didn't care. Without Darica, nothing really mattered anyway. I didn't understand how our lives had gone so crazy.

First, we found out we couldn't have kids; then my wife left me because the treatments didn't work. It seemed like every time we had a little bit of hope, something else happened. I was prepared to give anything to go back in time and be happy again.

My phone was once again ringing off the hook because I refused to answer for anyone, not even my own mother. I knew she would just show up here if I kept this up, so I vowed to pick up the phone the next time it rang, and it did. It was Nolan.

"Yeah."

"You doing okay, bruh?" he asked.

"No. My wife hasn't come home in a week. She's upset, depressed, and irrational. She won't go to work, and she isn't sleeping, eating, or checking in with me."

"How do you know what's going on with her, then?"

"She's over there with her mother, thank God."

"That's good. At least she has someone looking after her."

"It's not good for me. I want my wife back. I've never been away from her in the five years we've been married."

"She loves you. She'll be back."

"I feel like this is all my fault."

"Don't do that to yourself, bruh. There's nothing you could've done to prevent this. Why don't you let me talk to her?"

"I don't think she'll go for that."

"She already doesn't like me. What do we have to lose?"

"You got a point there."

Nolan

I contemplated whether I should show up at Darica's mother's house unannounced but decided against it. Minutes later, I was calling her from a blocked number. Her phone rang four times, and I was prepared to hang up when she picked up.

"What!" she yelled.

"Hello, Darica."

"How can I help you?"

"I just want to talk to you."

"I don't think that's a good idea," she said angrily.

"Can we meet for lunch tomorrow?"

"No."

"Please. I'll only take a few minutes to say what I have to say."

"Okay. Where?"

"My place. Do you remember where I live?"

"Yes."

"Great. I'll see you around twelvish?"

"Yes. See you then."

At around eleven thirty the next day, I was excitedly setting up the Monopoly game. I knew how much Darica loved it, and I couldn't wait to see her face light up when she laid her eyes on it. Seconds later, she arrived in a foul mood. The frown on her face instantly turned into a smile once she walked into my game room.

Darica

Everything inside me was screaming, "Tell him to cut to the chase and say what he has to say," but I loved the game so much that beating him seemed like the most important thing at the moment.

We played for hours, stealing glances at each other like old school friends trying to get to know each other again.

"I feel so rude."

"Why?" Nolan asked.

"The whole time I've been here, we've been playing Monopoly. I never thought to ask you what you'd like to do."

Nolan gave me a grin that pulled at my heartstrings for some reason, paused for what seemed like forever, and said, "I like to make up my own games."

"Okay. What do you have in mind?"

"The song game."

"How do you play it?"

"Instead of talking, you use a song or its lyrics to describe what's on your mind."

"That's hard."

"No, it's not. There's a song for everything. I'll go first. 'Nothing Compares To You,'" he sang.

"That's sweet."

"Don't say it, sing it," he reminded me.

"*Sweetest Thing I've Ever Known,*" I sang.

Nolan gave me a thumbs-up, then sang, "*That's What Friends Are For.*"

"*Anytime You Need a Friend, I will be here,*" I added.

We played Nolan's game until we ran out of songs. There were only so many songs you could sing about friendship, and love songs weren't appropriate for us.

"Are you hungry?" he asked.

"I'm starving. What did you get us to eat?"

"I didn't buy anything. I cooked."

"You can't cook."

"Have you forgot about that fancy breakfast I cooked for you a few months ago?"

"Anyone can cook breakfast."

"Well, you'll just have to taste my gourmet lunch and decide for yourself," Nolan said as he escorted me into the kitchen. He scooped up a heaping forkful of Beef Bourguignon and fed it to me.

I tasted the succulent entrée and closed my eyes as if it were the most exquisite thing that ever touched my tongue. I swished it around in my mouth and lingered on the taste before reluctantly swallowing it. After devouring most of my meal, I complimented Nolan on his skills in the kitchen.

"This tastes like it was cooked in heaven."

"I like you," Nolan chuckled. "You're the first person who's ever described my food like that."

"I'm not kidding. This is better than the food at SeaBreeze."

Nolan smiled and brought his food to the table. We ate in silence until we consumed everything.

"Think you can watch a movie without falling asleep?" he asked me.

"I can try," I said as he pulled out my chair, escorted me into the den, grabbed my hands, and massaged each finger as he admired the color on my neatly manicured nails. He then took off my shoes and rubbed my feet. I started nodding off, so he stopped and poured me a cold glass of water.

"Thank you," I said.

"For?"

"For showing me a good time and not demanding anything in return."

"Actually, I do want something in return."

"What is it?" I said inquisitively.

"I need to ask you to go light on my brother. He loves you and wants the best for you."

"I knew he put you up to this."

"No. I did it on my own. I wanted to make things right between you two. He doesn't even know about this."

I eyed him suspiciously, then regarded what he said. "Are you sure you're not doing this for Dolan?"

"No. I'm doing it for you. I know how badly you want a baby, and so does Dolan. I don't care how we raise that money; we're going to get it so you can continue those treatments."

"That's awfully sweet of you. I want to apologize for the things I said about having sex with you. I didn't mean to hurt your feelings."

"I'm not offended at all. I know exactly how you feel."

"How could you possibly know? You've never been married."

"But I was close."

"What?"

"Contrary to popular belief, I've been in love before. Love so strong that I was weak, so strong that I would never ever consider or regard making love to another woman."

"You?"

"Yes, me. Our situation was similar to yours."

"Are you serious?"

"Yes. Only she was the one who couldn't bear children."

"Really?"

"Yes. I never shared my story with anyone, but if you don't mind me venting to you, I would like to get it off my chest."

"Okay," I said anxiously. I listened intently as Nolan told me about his first love, Sheila, how they loved each other so much that they considered marriage but put it on hold to concentrate on having a baby.

"At first, she didn't know she couldn't conceive, but after months and months of trying, she noticed that she wasn't getting pregnant, so we went to a specialist who eventually informed us that she couldn't bear children. I told her I didn't care, that my love for her was so strong that it didn't matter if we never have children. She, on the other hand, was consumed with it. It seemed like every time we looked around, someone was in our face with a baby, and she was heartbroken, devastated, and felt less than a woman, no matter how many times I assured her that she was all I needed."

"Why didn't you just adopt?" I asked.

"We considered it, but she became obsessed with having our own baby, insisting that we try everything imaginable, spending a fortune on treatments . . . only to hear the same thing over and over, that she would not be a mother."

As if the story wasn't heartbreaking enough, tears started to fall from Nolan's eyes. I reached up to wipe them away, held his hand, and urged him to go on.

"She killed herself."

"Oh my God. That's terrible," I said. "I'm so sorry."

"So am I. My associate had just suggested that we have someone else carry her eggs."

"That would have been great."

"I was on my way to tell her what he said, and once she agreed with me, I was going to propose, but I was too late. That's why I made sure that you guys knew about every method in the book. I never want anyone to give up their dream of having a family. I promise you I'll do everything in my power to make sure you do. I feel like that would be my way of honoring her."

"You are really sweet for cherishing her in all her flaws. She was a lucky woman. I'm sorry I judged you."

"That's okay," he smiled. "Well, enough about me. I already took up too much of your day. Just consider what I said, okay?"

"I already did. You're right. I shouldn't take it out on my husband. It's not his fault. I know he loves me and wants me to have everything I desire, including that baby. Thank you for showing me that."

"You're welcome," Nolan said as he swiped the rest of his tears, walked me to the door, gave me a kiss on the cheek, and asked, "Can we do this again tomorrow, same time?" He looked so hopeful and vulnerable after telling his story that I just couldn't say no.

"That depends on what you're cooking."

"Anything you want."

"Monopoly too?"

"Of course."

"It's a deal."

I drove to my mother's house excited, suddenly feeling better about the situation and more optimistic about conceiving for the first time in months. Once I reached my destination, I called my husband.

"Hey, 'Every,' I've been worried sick."

"I know, 'Firsty.' I'm sorry. I shouldn't have snapped at you."

"It's okay, baby. I know you're under a lot of pressure. I miss you like crazy, though."

"I miss you too."

"I can't wait to see you tonight."

"I'm going to need a few more days."

"What? I thought you weren't mad."

"I'm not. I just need a few more days to regroup."

"O . . . o . . . Okay. Take as much time as you need," Dolan said reluctantly. I knew he missed me and wanted me home with him.

"Thanks, honey. I'll call you and keep in touch. It'll be like I'm there."

"Okay, baby. Did you talk to Nolan?"

"Yes. He called and told me to go easy on you." I didn't have the guts to tell my husband I spent the day with his brother.

"Did it work?"

"Of course, it did. That's why I called you."

"I'm glad."

"I am too. Talk to you soon, okay?"

"I love you."

"Love you more," I sang as I hung up the phone.

Moments later, my phone rang again. It was April.

"Hey, chica," I chimed.

"Hey, girl. You okay? You were pretty mad the other day."

"I'm good. I'm so sorry I went off on you. I know you were only trying to help."

"It's cool. I know I can be over the top sometimes. My alcoholic ass needs a muzzle. Have you talked to your husband?"

"Yes. I just got off the phone with him. I told him I'm not ready to go home. I haven't been back to work either."

"Take your time, sweetie. It's a tough thing to go through, I'm sure. Sorry this is happening to you guys. Folks that can love a child and provide a good home for it seem to have the hardest time sometimes. Thank God you have

Nolan. Most men would be offended by what you said, but not only is he understanding, he went out of his way to make sure you can continue those treatments."

"What do you mean? We're not doing the treatments. We still can't afford them."

"Oops. Forget I said that."

"April, what are you hiding?"

"I'm sorry. I thought you knew already."

"Knew what?"

"That Nolan took out a big loan so you can continue the treatments. I have a friend that works at his bank, and she told me about it. I feel terrible spilling the beans. Please don't tell him."

"I won't. I really had him twisted. He is one of the most beautiful people I've ever met."

"He sure is. I really wish his fine ass was interested in me. But he told me when all this is over, he's going back to claim this woman he's crazy about."

"Really?"

"That has to be the luckiest bitch alive."

"I agree. She's getting the cream of the crop, for sure."

"Anyway, chica, I have to go. My lunch break is over, and you know how my boss gets when I'm late."

"Have a good rest of the day, sissy. I love you."

"I love you more."

Evette

I waited in a rental car down the street from Nolan's house. He had shunned me weeks ago, and I was really starting to miss him. The longest we'd ever stayed away from each other in the past year was one week. Nolan could never resist my sexy body and beautiful face, but the way he was acting these past few weeks, I knew I was losing him.

From the first moment I laid eyes on the man, I knew he was my future. He was intelligent, handsome, and flashy, and I was his female counterpart. Both of us were dressed to the nines on a daily basis, both were scholars, and both the epitome of class. We hit it off from day one.

Nolan thought it was a coincidence that we got together, but our union was carefully orchestrated since the day I arrived at Daddy's birthday party. Our eyes met as we reached for a glass of champagne at the same time. He flashed that perfect smile before heading off in the other direction. He had some basic bitch that he was hurrying to get back to, but I had already decided he was mine. I approached Daddy to let him know that I wanted him, and he had the audacity to tell me I couldn't have him.

"Evette, people are not objects that you can interchange at your whim. You're not entitled to have everything you see."

Since when? I thought. If you look up "spoiled" in the encyclopedia, my picture-perfect ass would be right beside it. Daddy had been spoiling me since we found out about his bastard child. Well, actually before that, but he *really* laid it on thick when it was revealed.

"He's with a woman." Daddy nodded at a crowd of people Nolan was standing with.

"That little peasant?"

"The best I can do is introduce you and set up a date or two."

"You're chief of surgery, Daddy. He works for you. You can make him do anything you want."

"Evette, that's enough. I'll see what I can do."

"Make it happen, okay?" I said as I kissed him on the cheek.

"Nolan is going through some issues and has taken a leave of absence. I can't even influence him to come to work, let alone go out with you," he scowled as I gave him a look he couldn't resist. "Give me a week, and I'll see what kind of strings I can pull."

My daddy not only made it happen, but he also gave Nolan an offer he couldn't refuse. After two dates and a session at the park, I was convinced I had Nolan in the palm of my hand, our future was set, and he was head over heels in love. But it turned out he was insatiable and wanted other women, no matter how good I made him feel. I wore myself out trying to make his little problems disappear. It'd been over a year now.

Even though I could have had any man I wanted, I only had eyes for Nolan. He was my perfect match physically, mentally, and sexually. We loved to go out to the nicest clubs, eat at the finest restaurants, and make love in exotic places.

He made love to me like fire, touching and kissing me just the right way and making my body feel special. I wanted him to be my husband and the father of my children, and I wasn't giving him up without a fight. I would be horrified if any of those other bitches beat me to the punch. I already got rid of most of them. Now I had another issue . . . getting rid of the new one. I just had to figure out who she was.

Nolan didn't make it easy for me this time. He stopped going out, took a leave of absence from work, and was holed up in his house every day. I drove by his house three nights in a row but didn't see any cars in his driveway or on the street. I finally started passing by in the mornings and afternoons, hoping to luck up on something. For the past three days, I noticed one particular car parked in front of his house at approximately the same time.

I decided I was going to make a last-ditch effort to see who was driving that car. I knew in my heart that it belonged to the woman who was taking my baby's heart from me, and I wasn't about to sit here and allow it. I wanted to fight the bitch, kill the bitch, or at least hurt her bad enough to make her wish she never met Nolan. But I knew that wouldn't sit well with him. He hated violence. He saw enough of that in his line of work. He told me he sewed more ears, noses, and lips on than he cared to remember. If he had his way, he would make sure nobody ever had to lose a limb. I had a long list of ways to get rid of the other woman anyway, but that wasn't my concern at this particular point in time.

My heart beat with anticipation at noon when, just like clockwork, I saw the car pull up in front of the house, and a woman got out of it and make her way up the walkway.

She was wearing a simple black sundress and low heels; her flowing hair and voluptuous curves moved like she was doing a video shoot. She wore no jewelry, and her clothes weren't made by any known designer, but her perfect bone structure and unique body made me look like a charity case. I was hating the fact that she was knocking on his door and so jealous that I wanted to shoot her in the back to stop her from going in.

Nolan opened the door, gave her a winning smile and a tight hug, and kissed her on the forehead. He looked like he was going to fuck the shit out of her and forget about pulling out. I held my stomach in pain. I'd never seen Nolan greet anyone like that, and I felt like my competition was winning his heart. I almost screamed in agony when he gazed at her butt that looked like you could sit a cup on it, grabbed her hand, and escorted her into his world. The world *I* was supposed to be sharing with him.

Chapter Eight

Darica

"Surprise!" I yelled to Nolan as soon as he opened the door. I was fifteen minutes early.

"Hey, early bird," he said as he hugged me and escorted me in, thinking I missed the part where he looked at my butt. I chalked it up to the fact it was a man thing and let it go as I took in the aroma of meat sauce and cologne.

"Mmmmm, something smells good. What did you cook today?"

"None of your business, nosy. I see you got here early so you can catch me slipping. Just for that, you're going to wait until I bring it out."

"If it tastes anything like it smells, I'm in for a treat."

"Your suspense is almost over. It's done so we can eat right now. Sit at the table. I'll bring it to you."

I took off my sweater and sat at the dining room table as I was instructed. Nolan brought the food out, but he had it covered, so I still didn't know what I was about to eat. He took a large cloth napkin and tied it around my eyes.

"What's this all about?"

"It's a surprise," he said.

"Damn, man, do you have to make things so complicated?"

"You know you like it," he said.

I raised my brow in amazement but didn't say anything, as I allowed him to tie the napkin even tighter around my eyes so I couldn't see his surprise lunch. I kept quiet because I didn't want any more delays in getting the food in my mouth.

Seconds later, I felt a fork gently poke my lips and slightly nudge my mouth open. I opened it to let him feed me. When I tasted the flavorful meat, I thought I was in heaven. I had never tasted anything so good in my life.

"Damn, you can cook. You missed your calling. You should have been a chef."

"I have to make sure the mother of my child stays healthy," he said as he fed me more.

I almost choked when he made that comment. The combination of being fed, blindfolded, and spoken to in that manner had me feeling strange. I wasn't even pregnant yet, and he was talking like a proud baby daddy but also acting like my man. To top it off, he was acting like he forgot that the baby technically wouldn't be his Dolan's and mine.

After he fed me every morsel, he gave me a peck on the lips that instantly made me wet. Then he took the blindfold off and started seductively eating his own meal. I was going to return the favor and feed him, but after that kiss, I knew that was a bad idea. It didn't stop me from fantasizing that it was my juices landing on his tongue, though. I instantly wanted to kick myself.

Damn me. This is my brother-in-law. I shouldn't be thinking like this.

"Um . . . Can you excuse me? I need to call my husband," I told him.

"No problem," he said as he continued eating. "I'll meet you in the den. I found a great movie you're going to love."

As I walked to the patio to make the call, everything in me said, "Get the hell out of there." But I decided to stick it out a little longer. After all, I liked his company, and lunch and a movie was pretty harmless, right?

Dolan didn't answer, so I called his phone again. This time he answered, and I heard loud music. He didn't say anything, so I figured he accidentally answered the phone. I wondered why he was in such a noisy place in the middle of the day. I hung up figuring he would see the missed calls and get back with me soon, but I made a mental note to tell him to be more careful with his phone.

When I got to the patio, I let out a deep breath of relief for the escape from Nolan, but I wasn't happy about the unexpected sounds coming from Dolan's phone. I was going to go home tonight, but now, I wasn't so sure. I decided to go into the den and wait for Nolan to start the movie, but when I got halfway there, I heard screaming, yelling, and stiletto heels walking on the hardwood floor.

"Get out of my house before I call the police, Evette."

"Go to hell, Nolan. I've been with you for a year, and you do *this* to me?"

"That's just it. You've been with *me* for a year. I *haven't* been with you. What we had was nothing more than sex. Now, get the fuck out of my house."

"I'm not going anywhere until I see that bitch!" she screamed.

"Evette, don't make me—" he yelled, then instantly changed his tune when he saw me standing in the room.

"I'm sorry about this," he said sweetly as he looked over at me.

"No problem. Is everything okay?"

"Who does this bitch think she is coming out here asking if everything's okay?"

"First of all, you don't know me like that, so you need to back off. Don't get fucked up."

"Come on, bitch!" she yelled as she took off her earrings and shoes.

"Nolan, you better get your girl because I'm *not* the one!" I yelled.

"This bitch can get it today because I'm not sharing my man with nobody."

"I think you got it twisted, little mama. I'm *not* your man."

"You would say anything to keep fucking this bitch."

"That would be difficult since this woman is my sister-in-law," Nolan blurted as he opened up his wallet and pulled out Dolan's and my wedding picture.

"Oh my God," Evette gasped. "I feel so stupid. Please forgive me."

"It's cool," I said.

"She's just waiting for her business partner to arrive," he lied, knowing that Evette had been snooping around and spotted my car in front of his house the past couple of days. "She's my interior decorator, and this is the best time for them to do their magic."

"Forgive me, miss. I've been under a lot of pressure since he left me."

"That's understandable. I hope you guys can work it out," I said as I stared daggers at Nolan.

"Evette, I'll call you later," he told her.

"Please do," she said apologetically as she exited the house.

"Why didn't you tell me you were in a relationship with someone?"

"I'm not in a relationship with Evette, but she thinks I am."

"What did you do to make her think that?"

"Nothing. I made it very clear to her that I had needs," he said as he looked at me longingly. "Needs that hadn't been fulfilled in a long time," he stressed. "She agreed to handle them with no strings attached. I haven't touched her in weeks, though."

I swear, that look was intended for me, but I couldn't understand why he thought that was my concern, so I turned on the movie to change the subject. It didn't help that the movie was a romantic one, and I began to feel the familiar need for affection. Eventually, my body reacted in another way, and I started yawning. The heavy meal had made me sleepy, and I dozed off and woke up minutes later with my head in Nolan's lap.

"I'm sorry," I said. "That food gave me the itis."

"No problem. Can you excuse me?" he said, as he damn near threw me off the couch trying to get away from me.

I saw the imprint of his rod protruding through his pants as he was turning to walk away, but I couldn't dwell on it because my phone started ringing, and it was the call I was waiting for from Dolan. I excused myself onto the patio to take the call.

I said hello, but no one said anything back. I listened for a few seconds and heard my husband's voice. I couldn't believe my ears. He was talking to some woman. I had to take the phone off my ear to check that the call was actually from him.

"You are beautiful but—" I heard Dolan say.

"Fuck me, Dolan," the woman cut him off.

I heard the muffled sounds of moans, clothes being unfastened, and belt buckles clinking right before the call was disconnected. I was horrified. I had been defiant and gone absent, but that had never caused my husband to step out on me before. I knew he thought my behavior was immature and uncalled for, but he seemed to be cool when we talked. I didn't think he would do anything this drastic. But if he wanted to fuck over all we had with some hooker, so be it. Fighting over a man was never my thing, and it definitely wasn't an option. I wasn't going anywhere near home, and I damn sure wasn't going to my mother's house to mope.

I marched down the hallway to look for Nolan and tell him I was leaving to go to a hotel when I heard noises coming from his room. At first, I thought he was hurt . . . until I got close enough to peer through the slightly open door. He was lying on his bed with his head held back, hand wrapped tightly around his swollen erection, pleasuring himself.

I had never seen anything like this up close, only in magazines and the Pornhub site April liked to visit. Even then, I was ashamed to watch until the end. A part of me was insulted that he was doing this while I was here, and the other half was fascinated that he had the gall to please himself in spite of the circumstances. I wanted to say something but remained frozen like a deer in headlights.

He did say he was a man with needs, and he sure made a believer out of me. I still thought he had a lot of nerve for going at it during my visit when he could have easily waited until I left, but it was his house, and he could do whatever he wanted in it. I didn't want to leave without saying goodbye, but he was having way too much fun for me to ruin it. I turned to walk away.

Nolan

I smelled her exotic perfume before I saw her, and my eyes flew wide open. The first thing I saw was her hardened nipples showing through the delicate fabric of her dress. She was turning around to leave, but I knew she had to be curious about what she was watching me do. I couldn't let her walk away with the image of me getting myself off on her brain all night. Besides, if she really wanted to go, she would have hauled ass faster than that. I could tell from her mannerisms that she was fascinated by the act and wanted more.

"Wait!" I shouted. "Don't go."

"W . . . w . . . What do you want?" she asked shakily.

My eyes said it all. "Forgive me," I said to no one in particular as I stroked myself harder, using the visual aid in front of me. I was willing to bet anything that Darica was throbbing like a heartbeat between her legs, and she was going out of her mind right about now. She wanted me so badly; she couldn't even formulate a complete sentence, let alone make a reasonable decision.

"Come here," I demanded. She walked over to me without hesitation. I pulled her down on top of me and kissed her. This was, without a doubt, the sweetest kiss I'd ever tasted, and I urged her to lie down beside me and spread her legs. She obeyed.

I rolled on top of her and aggressively pushed myself against her opening. She felt so good that I almost exploded right then and there. It took everything in me to keep from losing it. I hadn't even penetrated her, and the pleasure was like nothing I've ever experienced. Imagine what it would be like if I filled her to capacity.

The thought of stopping crossed my mind, but I knew I wouldn't be able to make any reasonable sense with my mind, while my body was going crazy for hers. She had other plans.

I felt both her hands grab my chest and push me off her with all her might.

"We can't do this. I'm going to get a room," she said as tears rolled down her face.

"I'm sorry if I hurt you."

"It's not you. It's Dolan."

"What did he do?"

"I heard him and a woman . . ."

"What?"

"On the phone. I heard both of them having sex."

"What the hell was he thinking?"

"I don't know, but I'm not going back home or to my mother's. I'll call you when I get to the hotel."

"You're not staying at some hotel when you can stay here. I have plenty of room here. Besides, I can't let you leave in this condition. I feel guilty because he's my brother."

"You knew about this?"

"No, but I know my brother can be a little messy sometimes. He knows how hard we're working toward this baby. I would think he would act civilized at a time like this. Take the room down the hall." I pointed. She grabbed her purse and obeyed.

At around three in the morning, I heard her crying and immediately walked to her room. She had the door closed, so I knocked.

"Come in," she said as she covered her half-naked body with a blanket.

"You okay?"

"No," she cried. "It hurts bad."

I walked over, hugged her, and allowed her to cry on my shoulder. She smelled so good. I turned her around and cupped her. Even with the sheet as a barrier, I felt the heat coming off of her body. I looked down at my current attire and wanted to kick my ass for not pulling a pair of sweats over my boxers and a wife beater over my bare chest. My little man was excitedly poking her in her back side. He had had a taste of her and wanted more. But he would have to wait. Right now, she needed to be comforted. She melted into me, accepting the embrace.

Darica

I woke up with Nolan sleeping next to me, wishing like hell I wasn't in this predicament, and it was Dolan instead. The man was so handsome that I would've been happy tracing the lines of his face. I entertained the thought for a second, then thought better of it and turned to get out of bed.

"Don't go," he pleaded.

"What?"

"I want you," he begged.

"I can't."

He ignored me and started kissing me. They were some of the sweetest kisses I ever tasted. He pushed his tongue inside my lips, and they parted for him without hesitation. Something told me to run, that he was just using me for his own carnal pleasure. I thought about Dolan and the woman he had sex with, then thought of Nolan and how he was turning me on.

By now, he had my left breast in his mouth sucking on my nipple like a hungry child. I couldn't believe I was doing this.

I moaned from the intense pleasure as my lower lips became wet with my juices and started thumping from need. Dolan and I hadn't had sex much because of the stress of trying to get pregnant and, even before that, the pressure of trying to conceive took away some of the pleasure. I wasn't having that problem right now. Nolan had me ready to grab his big, beautiful organ and put him deep inside of me.

"Oooooooh," I cried. "I want you so bad."

"I'm yours. Take me," he whispered.

I inched away, and he pulled me back. The head of his dick was at my opening.

"Nooooooooo, pleeeeeeease," I begged. "We can't do this. You're my—"

"Shhhhh," he interrupted. "The only thing I am to you right now is a man who can give you pleasure beyond your wildest dreams."

That statement alone made me cream on the sheets. Nolan must have felt it because the next thing I knew, he was pushing his very hot, extremely thick rod inside my tight walls . . . and I let him.

Nolan

If I ever thought I made love to a woman before, I was sadly mistaken. This was the motherfucking truth. It felt like love and lust, pain and pleasure, right and wrong—all at the same damn time.

Her tight walls were so warm and wet; yet they fit me like a glove, curving to my dick like a second skin.

"Fuuuucck!" I screamed. "You feel so good."

"So do you," she whispered in a barely audible tone. Her whole body was shaking as she opened up and received every throbbing inch of me, and she was yelling my name over and over like a beautiful prayer.

"Nolan . . . Oh my God, Nolan. Don't stop, Nolan. Yes, Nolan. Give me all of you, Nolan. Take me, Nolan."

I happily obliged.

Darica

He was deep inside me, and I could barely hang as he moved with the precision of a man making love for the very last time. Hurried, primal, forbidden. I pushed him away slightly, and he slowed down. At first, I thought he was going to give me a final chance to change my mind, but, no, he was only giving me enough time to adjust to his size.

My head wanted to stop him, but who was I kidding? My body never wanted it to end. Once he was completely inside me, he moaned like it was the best feeling in the world, paused, and started stroking me as if his life depended on it. I could tell he was trying desperately to make it last, but it was a struggle for him.

I heard noises, and it took me awhile to figure out that they were my own guttural moans echoing throughout the house. My body was going crazy, and I didn't have control of the sensations he was bringing me. I thought about pushing him off me a few more times, but just like the times before, I couldn't break free of his grip.

It was such an incredible feeling; I almost felt it was impossible to be real. The most powerful orgasm was building up inside me, and I couldn't wait for it to explode. In my heart, I knew it was wrong, but something was driving me that was more crucial than the pleasure he was giving me. I knew how important this culmination was to our future.

Nolan

We had only been at it for about fifteen minutes, but I knew I wouldn't be able to last much longer with the death grip her bomb-ass pussy had on my dick. I wanted to take a break on the fucking and taste her sweet honey, but I was afraid she would use it as an opportunity to call it quits. The next thing I knew, I was calling out her name. I knew I would hate myself for ever letting sounds escape from my mouth if I said the words I had waited forever to speak.

Lucky for me, the words came out as, "Darica, your pussy is so good. I've wanted you for so long. Please let this be real," instead of what I *really* wanted to say which was, "I love you, Darica. I never want to be without you, baby. Please stay with me forever."

If I didn't know any better, I would think that cupid and Karma had joined forces and shot my ass with some kind of bullshit that was created in a supernatural lab. I didn't even feel this way about Sheila, but here I was, losing my fucking mind over my sister-in-law.

Her title alone should have made me feel guilty and back away, but a sinister smile came across my face instead. It was an epiphany that came to me, and all of a sudden, nothing else mattered. The truth was this was an opportunity of a lifetime, and our unborn child was dying to be conceived.

"I'm about to come!" I screamed as I pumped my seeds deep inside a woman for the first time unprotected, and we came together in a mind-blowing orgasm. My whole body was shaking, and I grabbed her and held her tighter than I ever held anyone in my life. As a matter of fact, holding someone had never been my thing. I waited for her breathing to return to normal and kissed her on the lips.

She thought I was done, but I was bricked up and ready for more. I carried her to the chaise lounge, put one foot on top of it, flipped that ass over, and entered her from the back, pushing every inch of my manhood inside her. I went in so deep, I shocked the hell out of her, and she gasped. A few minutes later, I felt her pushing back.

She was throwing it back so strong, that she made me lose my bearings. I usually lasted longer during round two, but she quickly dispelled that myth. The next thing I knew, I was coming again, with an even larger load than earlier. Now, *that* was a first. This time when I delivered my seed, it knocked the wind out of me.

We fell asleep in each other's arms.

Dolan

"What the hell is wrong with you, Miko? You know I'm married."

"You're not acting like a married man. I didn't force you to come to my place."

"I came to talk."

"That's not what your friend down *there* wanted to do."

"I had too much to drink and passed out. Get up off me. I don't want your ass."

"You could have fooled me," she said angrily. "I heard you and your wife were having problems."

"Well, you heard wrong."

"What do you see in her anyway? It's obvious she doesn't love you. Every time I look around, she's with your brother."

"My brother is helping us with something."

"You're so stupid; you can't see your brother's in love with your wife. If you don't watch yourself, she's going to be in love with him too."

"You're just talking that shit because you want me. Did you do the same thing with him?"

"His little girlfriend made it very clear that he belonged to her, but that bitch ain't talking all that shit since he left her."

"What are you talking about?"

"Evette. He was fucking her on a regular basis until you and your wife started hanging out with him. Then, he dropped her like a hot potato. It doesn't matter what I did with Nolan. I've always wanted you, Dolan."

"Sorry. The feeling's not mutual. Didn't I tell you to move out of my way?"

"You better treat me nice, or I'll tell your wife everything about us."

"She won't believe shit you say. It's not like you're the most reputable person around."

"She already heard part of it, so it'll be easy to convince her of the rest."

"Just get out of my way. Forget you ever met me."

"I'll be waiting for you to come crawling back to me."
"Don't hold your breath."

Nolan

I woke up with a feeling of complete satisfaction and happiness in my soul. I had never felt this way about making love to anyone, and, needless to say, my judgement was clouded by the love that was pent-up inside me for God knows how long. I did not doubt in my mind that she was ovulating because this was the time of the month the doctors indicated she always did. I was sure that she was pregnant already, and if she weren't, she would be by the time I was done with her tonight.

Darica

I stirred, smiled, stretched, opened my eyes, looked at Nolan, and jumped. I was sure I dreamed the whole event as I did countless times before, and when I would wake up, I would be alone in bed, forced to deal with my guilt, but, nevertheless, happy it was only a fantasy. The soreness in my body told me that we most definitely went to the next level.

"Oh my God, Nolan. What have we done?"

"I think we made a baby," he smiled.

"Oh no."

"What do you mean, *no?* Isn't this what you wanted? This should be the happiest day of your life."

"I didn't want it like this. This is wrong."

"You weren't saying that when I was deep inside you."

"I couldn't help myself then."

"But you want to take it back now? I was hoping we could do it a few more times to seal the deal."

"Seal the deal?"

"Yes. I want to come in you a few more times to make sure you get pregnant."

"I don't think that's a good idea, Nolan. We shouldn't have done this," I said as I frantically looked for my clothes.

"Are you insane? I think this is the most beautiful thing in the world. You act like it's the most horrific."

"I think I should go get a morning-after pill."

"We've spent thousands on treatments, and now that we did it naturally and increased our chances, you want to get rid of my baby?" he scowled.

"We don't even know if I'm pregnant."

"I'm pretty sure you are."

"I have to go," I said. I was sick to my stomach.

"No."

"What?"

"I said no. I've given my life so you can have a baby, and now that I know there's a possibility you're carrying my child, there's no way I'm going to risk losing it. Sit down and make yourself comfortable, ma," he said as he pushed me backward.

I landed on the bed. "So, now you're going to rape me?"

"I don't have to. From now on, you belong to me."

"You arrogant son of a bitch," I said as I held my head. I felt a migraine coming.

"Watch your mouth."

"Why is this happening?"

"This is destiny. It's meant to be. We don't always get to choose the perfect life."

"You're talking like a crazy person. All I wanted was a baby."

"That's what you're going to get. Just relax and let me help you. If we do it your way, this thing will drag on forever."

I wanted to protest, but I realized he had a point. "Okay. Let's talk about it."

He gave a smile of relief.

"Can I get you anything to make you comfortable?"

"No, thank you."

"First off, you need to call Dolan and your mother and check in with them," he ordered.

"I'll call my mother, but I don't have anything to say to Dolan."

"Suit yourself. But get yourself together. We have unfinished business."

"I told you I felt funny about doing this. Now that I'm not with my husband, I don't even know if I want to have a baby."

"Yes, you do because you realize this is a once-in-a-lifetime opportunity. You've wanted a baby for five years. You could already be pregnant from me making love to you twice, but we need to be realistic and do it the entire time you're ovulating, to make sure you conceive. Don't let Dolan mess this up for you."

"If I decide to divorce him, having a child will only complicate things. Besides, I was only doing this for my husband. But now that he's having trouble keeping his dick in his pants, he doesn't deserve a baby. I'd rather have a baby with a man who can be faithful to me."

"I agree with you, but when is that going to be? Huh? When you find a new man? After a messy divorce?"

I squinted my eyes shut and shook my head. I hated Nolan for saying that, but I had to admit he had a point. It could take years to get divorced and find love again . . . if ever. I wanted to be a mother right now. Nolan could give me the baby, and we could all walk away with no strings. Nolan had said he didn't want to have any responsibilities and signed paperwork to prove it. I'd already had sex with him. What would a few more times hurt?

"Okay. We can have sex a few more times to ensure my conception but don't forget that this is still a business transaction. And keep this on the hush. As far as they know, we got lucky with the treatments."

"The secret's safe with me. Let me know when you're ready for round three."

Nolan

I was glad Darica came to her senses. If she wouldn't have agreed to my terms, I was prepared to hold her hostage in this house for three days, so that she wouldn't get that morning-after pill. But I knew that would've only caused her to resent me, and there wouldn't be a chance in hell she would lie down with me again. My brother had no idea how he messed up a good woman by fucking around with the next top thot. He needed a lesson in treating a woman like a queen. For the next three days, I was going to do just that.

Miko

When I looked through my photo album, I couldn't help but smile as I showed my therapist the pictures.

"I hope I can help you," she said. "Tell me what happened." She rubbed my arm and smiled.

"Me and Dolan hit it off so good in junior high school; I was sure we'd be married by now. We started off as best friends, but he had a crush on me for months and decided to ask me out. On the day we were supposed to go, Dolan decided to hit up Nolan's friend, Trent, for a loan. Trent was a lot more advanced than Dolan. He was already getting girls, most of them older than him, and he made it no secret that he was all about the sex. My hormones were out of whack, and I couldn't understand why I wanted to be with so many guys. If I had my way, I would be with Dolan and a couple of other boys too. I was pretty and well filled out for my age, with the body of a grown woman. Do you think I'm a nympho?"

"We'll get to that later. Go on with your story."

"That summer, the plumbing went out at my house, and I asked Dolan if I could take a bath at his. The answer, of course, was yes, and he provided me with a facecloth and towel. I relaxed in the hot bubble bath a bit, then washed completely as thoughts of my handsome crush, Dolan, innocently lodging in the next room, consumed me. My fingers traveled to my vaginal lips, and I closed my eyes and let my fingers travel to my mature button. I rubbed myself until I cried out and almost released when a plan formulated in my brain. I unplugged the drain, grabbed my towel, placed it around my wet body, and walked into Dolan's room where he was playing video games.

"He smelled the fresh bubble bath on my body before he saw me and looked up into the eyes of a woman who was ready to be taken. I sat on his lap, and all the water from my body drenched his clothes. I kissed him, swirling my sweet tongue in his mouth and felt his penis rise into his sweats. He dropped the remote control he was using to play the game. It fell on the floor and cracked. I dry humped him until I felt my sweet release, and he didn't get to make me a woman. He'd made it in his pants and was trying to recuperate when I jumped up, put on my sundress and sandals, and ran out of his house. My hair and body were still damp."

"Was this the day you two fell out?"

"No. As a matter of fact, there were several opportunities where we found ourselves alone in his room, grinding on each other with our clothes on. We had our fun, but we knew it wasn't time to go to the next level.

"But later that summer when Dolan came to Trent's house, he heard voices and figured his friend or brother had talked some girl into going all the way once again. He opened the door to Trent's room, figuring maybe he could get a peek or at least some pointers. He was horrified at the sight."

"What happened?" she asked, looking like she was on the edge of her seat.

"He found me grinding on Nolan. Both of us were moaning and groaning and going at it something fierce. He knew I wasn't merely entertaining Nolan with one of my infamous dry hump sessions because Nolan had his manhood deep inside me, with at least three inches hanging out. He could see where I had wet most of his brother's penis with my juices and was trying to get the rest of it inside me. Dolan bolted out of the room, anger filling his body. We were so engrossed that we never noticed him.

"Needless to say, Dolan never took me out again. He had sex with one of my hungry friends to get back at me. He could never bring himself to forgive me for betraying him and messing up his first time. But I always wanted him, always put everything into getting his love, always wondered what could have been if I hadn't let my hormones get the best of me the day I got with Nolan.

"Now with Darica out of the picture, I feel like I have a second chance. I always told Dolan he was never meant to be with her anyway. I knew it was only a matter of time before she would divorce him."

"Are you sure it's over between them? I don't want you in the middle of a love triangle. Maybe you need to focus on just being his friend."

"I don't want to be his fucking friend. I want to be his wife."

"But he's already married."

"I thought you were supposed to help me."

"I'm trying to, but we don't want to play a part in wrecking a marriage. I would like to see you in a healthy relationship, instead of the ones where you just end up in bed with someone."

"I wouldn't do that if I had Dolan."

"Well, we need to take baby steps for now. I'll see you next week, and we can talk about your promiscuity."

"Okay, Doctor. Thank you," I said as I grabbed my purse and my appointment card from her.

The current trip down memory lane made me long for my baby so badly that I decided to call him, hoping to catch him in a good mood.

"What!" Dolan blurted.

"You want to grab something to eat?"

"Are you crazy? I told you to leave me alone. I don't want nothing to do with you."

"Why are you so mean to me? I just want to hang out with you."

"You're full of shit. I don't have time, Miko."

"Look, Dolan, I understand you want your wife back. Just allow me to tell—"

"I don't want to talk to you or see you. Find one of your men friends to keep you company!" Dolan yelled into the phone before he hung up.

Rolanda

2004

We walked into the house to find both of our sons fighting like dogs on the street. My husband, Phillip, and I pulled them off each other and took them into separate rooms. I ended up in the den with Dolan, and Nolan went into the kitchen with Phillip.

"What the hell happened?" I wheezed.

"He took my girl," Dolan huffed.

"I didn't know you had a girl."

"She was my crush. I thought I meant something to her."

"If you meant something to her, then he wouldn't have been able to take her, right?" I pointed out.

"Yes. But he broke the code."

"What's the code?" I asked.

"You wouldn't understand, Ma."

"Try me."

"For one thing, he's my brother. We're supposed to be close. Your brother's woman is off limits. He went after her like he didn't care."

"You think it's all his fault?"

"No. But if it's not, he sure as hell didn't try hard to resist her."

"Let's get Nolan's story, okay?" I told him.

"Okay."

I was a little disturbed that my teenage sons were thinking about crushes, let alone having sex. I hoped Phillip had gotten a chance to have "the talk" with them about protecting themselves from diseases and unwanted pregnancies.

Phillip and Nolan walked out of the kitchen, and it looked like he was successful in calming Nolan down. Nolan appeared to be remorseful, but I needed to know his side of the story. Both of them had Brandon's traits, so making a distinction between who was innocent was a moot point.

"I knew Dolan was head over heels in love with Miko, but she's always been a fast one," Nolan said. "I wasn't checking for her, and I wasn't expecting her to come over to Trent's house that day, but she had never been mean to me, so I was civil to her. We actually had a decent conversation about school, the weather, and sports. The next thing I knew, I had fallen asleep on Trent's bed. The last time I saw him, he was on the phone with some skank, so I figured Miko had left or gone to the bathroom or something. I woke up to her grinding on me. I tried to push her off, but it was difficult. The ho was aggressive as all getout, and I could tell she wasn't going to leave without getting something out of the deal. I was going to play with her head, but it went too far. She had helluva tricks up her sleeve."

"Save the details," I said as I held my hand up. "So, what you're saying is this girl came on to you, and it got out of hand?"

"Yes. I would never have tried her on my own. I'm sorry, man. She is not for you or me."

"I guess it's a blessing in disguise," Dolan said. "Thanks, man. You did me a favor." He reached over to hug his brother like nothing ever happened. But as far as I knew, he never took his guard down after that.

Chapter Nine

Dolan 2014

"Happy birthday to you!" the crowd screamed.

I smiled, blew out my candles, and thanked everyone for their good wishes. I was especially thankful to see my wife. I had to beg her to come, but in the end, she gave in. Maybe it was because my mother, Rolanda, had been planning this party for months and spent a minifortune to put it together. Darica knew her absence from the event would be a red flag that our marriage was in trouble. We never missed any of Rolanda's events. It had been over a week since Darica left home, and she still hadn't told me why she refused to return.

I was surprised to see Nolan. He didn't like parties unless they were flashy and expensive with paparazzi and people wearing designer clothes. He believed a regular celebration was a waste of time and energy. For that reason, he never participated in any of our family functions. Many family members snubbed him because they felt he thought he was too good to hang out with them. Our mother thought it was great that he was trying to lose that black sheep image.

About the only one worse than Nolan was our half brother, Greg. He was invited to the party, but no one wanted him there because of his involvement with crazy women and the drama that followed him when he did come to family events.

His latest "baby mama" refused to cooperate with the paternity test because she said he *knew* he was the father (as if it was unheard of that she could possibly have had sex with someone else!). She was notorious for showing up at family functions with her mother and kids in tow. Greg's wife, Chevette, stayed close to our mother. She was hoping this was the one event Rella would not come to.

"Don't worry, honey," Rolanda said. "I don't think she'll turn up here to Dolan's party. She's not married to Greg, and she doesn't even talk to us. Let me find out who keeps telling her about our family gatherings, and they won't be invited to nothing else."

"Greeeeeeeeg!" Rella screamed as she walked into the kitchen with her 8-month-old daughter on her hip. Greg was in the backyard with some of his cousins.

"*Excuse* me?" Rolanda said.

"You're excused," she said as she rolled her eyes, handed her baby to her mother, and put her hand on her hip. "My daughter wants to see her daddy."

"You got me twisted walking in here like you were invited."

Before Rella could speak, her mother answered for her. "You sitting over here on your high horse like Greg and Chevette is a prince and princess. Y'all need to learn how to act around my daughter," she spat. "She should be treated like a queen because she has his children, so she comes first."

"What you need to do is get a DNA test and stop using that baby to control that man," Rolanda said to Rella. "It's obvious you don't have anything going for yourself, and nobody wants you. And your mama need to wash her crusty butt before she ever think about walking into this house uninvited again," she said as she threw her a bottle of lotion.

"Let's go, Rella."

"But my baby didn't get to see her daddy," Rella whined.

"We'll catch up with him later," her mama said.

"Okay," she agreed as they walked out, much to every-one's relief. Rolanda felt sorry for the baby, but she meant what she said about Rella.

"Anyone want more cake?" she asked to change the subject and lighten the mood.

I couldn't wait for the party to end, only because I wanted to talk to my wife, end any beef we had, and bring her back home. She was looking especially sexy today, and I couldn't wait to get her back home and in my arms.

My eyes followed her everywhere she went. She headed in the kitchen to get punch, then to the den to speak with my mother, and finally toward our bedroom. I wanted to follow her, but I knew she would curse me out if I did. She stayed in there about fifteen minutes, then came out with a large duffle bag.

I pleaded with my eyes, but she only rolled hers at me and headed out the door. *Oh shit,* I thought as I pushed past some family members to get to her, but she quickened her pace and ran out. By the time I got outside, she was in the car, preparing to drive away. I jumped in front of the car.

"Please don't leave. I can't be without you anymore."

"From the looks of things, you're doing a good job."

"Don't do this now, Darica. Come back inside. Give me a chance to talk to you after everyone leaves. If you still want to leave after that, you're free to go."

Darica got out of the car, closed the door, and walked back into the house.

I let out a deep breath, happy I had another chance to plead my case.

Nolan

I hated being here. I only came to see Darica. She kept her end of the deal and allowed me to make love to her for three more days. I used every trick in the book to convince her that we were making the right decision.

She seemed to be having the time of her life with me, but at the end of the agreed upon time, she quickly left my house and went to a hotel. I begged her not to go, even promised I wouldn't touch her because truth be told, I would've been happy just cuddling. But she was determined to get away from me.

Every time I looked at Dolan, I shook my head. He had fucked up big time, and I didn't feel he deserved his wife back. I was ecstatic when I saw Darica emerge from their bedroom with a duffle bag and storm out of the house, only to be replaced by disappointment when Dolan followed her and brought her back. I was hoping Darica wouldn't fall for any of my brother's shenanigans. But he always had that effect on women.

This made my job that much harder. I grew to love Darica and didn't want her to be used or abused. I was sure he fucked Miko, and there was no telling what kind of nasty disease she had. Miko wanted Dolan from the jump, and I felt they deserved each other. I was determined to help Darica all I could, especially if she was pregnant. She didn't need those problems.

I couldn't keep my eyes off of Darica. It was all I could do to keep from grabbing her and kissing her right then and there. She headed to the bathroom, and I followed her like a needy kid and quickly shut the door behind us.

"What the hell are you doing, Nolan?" she whispered.

"I just want to talk to you," I said as I locked the door.

"It can't wait until I pee?"

"Darica, what are you doing?"

"It's called 'using the bathroom.'"

"You know damn well what I'm talking about. I know you're not thinking about going back to him after he cheated."

"What I do with my husband is none of your business."

"It is if you're pregnant. You're going to be exposed to stress and all kinds of diseases. I don't want you going through that while you're carrying my baby."

"I appreciate your concern, but I can take care of myself."

"Think about what I said, Darica." She looked at me like I was crazy as I unlocked the door, opened it, made sure no one was around, and quickly closed the door behind me.

It wasn't my intent to commit such a heinous crime, and I had to admit, making love to my brother's wife was the lowest of the low. There was no way I could sugarcoat it and pretend that it was anything but insane; but somehow, I found beauty in it, embraced it, and fell in love. I wasn't proud of what I did, but when you danced with the devil, some things were just bound to happen.

I guess you could say day one, we took it slow. There was more foreplay than anything else. I set up the Monopoly game, and we played it for hours as if what we were about to do was the last thing that was going to happen. We moved on to the song game, acting as if we were old lovers and choosing more romantic categories.

I watched Darica talk to April and some friend named Nuni for hours as I busied myself with house chores as if it were our normal routine. I couldn't help but wonder if she was telling them what we had planned, and they tried to talk her out of it. I felt so comfortable with Darica; it felt like we were husband and wife. But I realized it was a struggle for her. I wanted her to feel at home, not like she was in a strange place so that she could get used to me. I wasn't in a rush, so I allowed her to take as much time as she needed.

I had grabbed some food at SeaBreeze, so I wouldn't have to worry about cooking. We ate our food in silence, both of us nervous at the idea of what we were about to do. At about ten p.m., I put on a comedy movie, massaged her shoulders, and handed her a drink. She was tense, so I urged her to relax.

"This will be easier if you let go," I whispered.

"What do you mean?" she asked.

"Well, most couples that conceive aren't this uptight. They're happy and worry free. When they make love, they're confident about conceiving. Even the ones who don't plan to get pregnant."

"I see," she said. She wasn't drinking fast enough, so I took the glass and brought it to her lips. After a couple of sips, I felt her loosen up.

"That's it. Go with the flow," I urged as I brought my mouth to hers and kissed her. To my surprise, she didn't fight me. She also allowed me to undress her without protesting. I carried her to my bed, and we made passionate love all night.

The following morning, I brought her breakfast in bed and fed her every morsel. I could tell she was a little nervous, but she did mostly everything I suggested. We made love in the shower, got dressed, and went to the beach. That day was more beautiful than any other day I remembered having in my life. We held hands as we watched the waves and the other couples in love. We fell right into place, even though we were living a lie. She seemed to be completely comfortable with me by the time we arrived back home. She offered to cook dinner and even fed me this time. It was the best lasagna I ever tasted. She seemed anxious to make love to me, and we went at it like beasts. The third night, I decided to kick it up a notch. It was my favorite. I hoped it was hers too. Darica talked a lot of shit, and I'm not gonna lie; she had me mad as hell when she told me to get to the business. She had the nerve to ask me if she had to go elsewhere to get her baby. What the fuck did she mean by that? I was determined to show her I was a man of my word. Not only did I fuck the hell out of her when I got her in bed again, but I also pulled out every trick in the book. By the time I was done with her ass, she was crying and shaking. How's *that* for a business transaction?

Dolan

It didn't take me long to notice that neither my brother nor wife was around. When I got up to investigate, I saw Nolan emerge from the hallway, but there was no sign of Darica. The things Miko said about them the other day had me thinking. What if Nolan had the hots for my sexy wife? What if Darica was mad enough to fall for his tricks? The thought of it made me hot under the collar, so I stormed into the hallway and confronted Nolan.

"Where's my wife?"

"I saw her take a phone call in the bedroom," Nolan said. I had a feeling he was lying.

"Thanks."

He knew something was wrong when I greeted him coldly and didn't use my traditional term of endearment, *man,* before or after I thanked him.

Darica came out of the bathroom. I could tell she was surprised to see her husband and brother-in-law standing there like we were both expecting something from her. I wanted my wife home. I didn't know what my brother wanted, but I sure wanted to find out.

Darica sensed something in the air. She smiled, pushed past us, and made her way into the living room where she sat with our cousins in the safe zone.

Rolanda

I didn't know what the hell was going on with my sons, but I wanted them to get their shit together . . . and do it fast. If they thought they could fool me, they definitely had another think coming. I made a call to Phillip who was running late to the party.

"Hey, my love," he answered.

"Hello, Phillip. Are you almost here?"

"Yeah. I'll be there in about fifteen minutes. Is everything okay?"

"No. I need you to talk to your sons. The tension between them is so thick, you could cut it with a knife."

"Okay. I'll get with them as soon as I can."

"For some reason, I feel it has something to do with some woman, and I hope like hell it's not Darica. She's acting strange too. If time allows, I plan to get her alone so I can get to the bottom of it. I have a feeling she knows something."

"Sit tight, baby. We'll figure it out together."

"Okay," I sighed.

After I hung up with Phillip, I turned my attention back to Chevette and felt sorry for her because she reminded me so much of myself when I was younger. I grabbed her hand that was resting on the table, and she looked relieved.

"Baby, you need to get tough. There's no way in hell a beautiful woman like you needs to allow Rella to walk in here and disrespect you like that."

"I don't know how to be tough."

"How long are you going to sit there and take this? There's not a man alive who is worth what he's putting you through."

"I love my grandson, but he needs his ass whooped for this one!" Mama C shouted. "My blood doesn't run through his veins, but I raised him, and I taught him better. I swear, some of the men in our family act just like Brandon and Landi's trifling asses instead of Phillip, who did everything in his power to make them real men."

"I'm leaving him," Chevette replied almost inaudibly.

I waited for Mama's response to see if she'd tell Chevette the same thing she told me so many years ago about running, but she didn't.

"Good. You deserve better than what you're getting. Everybody isn't lucky enough to land a Phillip, but you will have peace of mind eventually," Mama C assured her.

"I'm happy for you, Chevette. You are always welcome to stay with us until you get on your feet," I said as I pulled her in for a hug.

"Thanks. I might just take you up on your offer."

I thought about the year that Phillip and I were going through some troubles. Everybody always referred to him as a god, and I couldn't argue that he was a godsend. But he definitely wasn't a saint. It was at a time that Brandon was trying to get back with me. Yes, Brandon tried me again. He didn't give up, even after I married Phillip. I knew Phillip had people that watched me, and I was cool with that. But a woman will do what she wanted if she wanted to.

Brandon invited me to lunch, and my dumb ass went. It didn't take long for him to get on my nerves, and I stormed out of his house in a huff. Unfortunately, Phillip's reporters didn't see *that* part. I didn't care at the time. But I later realized Phillip was always insecure about the hold Brandon seemed to have on me.

He allowed that to make him turn to the women who promised they would do a better job pleasing him. Phillip was rich, and I knew women tried him all the time. I think he felt he was losing me, so he allowed a woman to get close to him, and before we knew it, she was trying to put a wedge between us.

I wasn't jealous nor was I upset. I had made my bed and was prepared to lie in it. But I wasn't going to give up my man without a fight. He meant too much to me. We had ten properties, twenty businesses, three kids, and one on the way. I knew, sooner or later, the bitch would surface. When she approached me, I was ready for her.

"Are you Ro?" she asked.

"Who's asking?"

"His woman, Renae."

"Those are some big panties to fill. You sure you can handle it?"

"I handle them very well," she spat.

"Do you know where he lives or what his net worth is?"

"I don't have to know. I have his baby growing inside me."

"Oh? How many months are you?"

"Two."

"Let me give you a piece of good advice. Phillip got a vasectomy the day he found out we were going to be parents five months ago—at my request. I'm six months pregnant, so unless you know something I don't, there's no way he could be the father of your baby. Now run along, little dummy."

Her bottom lip dropped so far down that I thought it was going to hit the ground.

That was the last time anyone ever heard from Little Miss Renae. I let Phillip know that the next woman that he fooled around with that had the nerve to step to me would be the last. I never had a problem with him again. If more women put their foot down, there would be fewer side chicks and more solid families. I prayed that Chevette would take me up on my offer of help because we were about to show Miss Rella how it was really done.

Darica

When the festivities were over, Nolan gave me a pleading look like he wanted to scoop me in his arms before reluctantly walking out the door to his car. I had a quick flashback of us laughing and playing like schoolkids, feeding each other, and making erotic love on those three days we were trying to conceive.

On day three, Nolan pulled out all the stops. He took me to a sky suite at the Aria, one of the most breathtakingly beautiful rooms I'd ever seen in my life. He bathed me, fed me, went down on me, and had me in positions I had never seen or heard of, while I enjoyed a panoramic view of the city.

"Stop fighting it, Darica," Nolan had begged.

I admit I was resistant in the beginning.

"I know you have feelings for me. You can't tell me you lay there and took that pounding I gave you and didn't feel anything, that I don't make your heart flutter or skip a beat every time you see me. Tell me that you don't get butterflies in your stomach when you think of me every day, and at the mere mention of my name, you don't get wet. You can't say you don't want to spend every waking moment with me and end your days and nights with me lying next to you. We have something special between us. I touch you in places your husband can't even dream of."

"Nolan, this is a business transaction, nothing more, nothing less, and I suggest you view it as just that. It'll be easier that way."

"Darica, can you just tell me the truth? If you can't be honest with me, can you at least be honest with yourself?"

"Nolan?"

"Yes?"

"Are you going to fuck me or what?"

"What?"

"Are you going to give me my baby, or do I have to go elsewhere?"

"Well, damn," he said. "You're really gonna do this?" I could see the hurt in his eyes, but I didn't care. There was only one goal of this union, and that was to make a baby. I had a husband, and even though he cheated, I felt like we would work things out eventually. I still wanted to do things the same way using Nolan as the donor, and even if Dolan and I got a divorce, split everything fifty-fifty, and shared custody, it would all be worth it in the end.

If I did owe anyone loyalty, it was Dolan. He was my husband. Nolan was my brother-in-law, a single man. One who could have any woman he wanted and children of his own one day. For all I knew, he only wanted me because I was a challenge, and once he got what he wanted, he would bounce. His eyes told me his feelings went deeper, and I was sorry he caught feelings for me, but I couldn't give him anything in return. I knew that was our last night together, and to be honest, I felt I deserved to be treated special. So I let down my guard and allowed him to say his piece and do anything he wanted to my body.

He laid a towel down, poured wine in my navel, and sucked it out, spilled champagne in the V of my love and slurped it out of every crevice, placed whipped cream and chocolate syrup on my breasts, and licked both peaks until they were as hard as pebbles. He made love to me like a man who had just gotten out of an insane asylum and kissed me like a man who was madly in love. The man knew how to work a woman over.

If I were single and dating, I probably would have made him my one and only and been ready to get down on one knee to propose to *him*. I definitely understood why he had the women going crazy for him. But I had other plans, and he did not fit into them.

I realized how detrimental my thoughts were, so I shook myself out of my contemplations, finished up my glass of wine, and went into the den to talk to my husband.

"Finally alone," Dolan sighed as he escorted me to the couch, sat me down, and grabbed my hands. "Come home to me, baby."

"Home?" I laughed. "You can forget that."

"What? Why?"

"Don't play with me, Dolan. You fucked another woman."

"Never."

"You're a liar. Move out of my way."

"What the fuck? I didn't cheat."

"I have to go," I said as I pushed past him.

"Not until you explain to me what happened."

"I don't have to explain shit!" I yelled as I got up, grabbed my purse, and stormed out the door. I jumped in my car, sped off, and made my way to my hotel room, ignoring the calls coming from my cell phone. I tried to tell myself that because of the nature of my "business transaction," I was not guilty. That Dolan was more accountable because of the way he cheated and who he did it with. I used the need for a baby to justify my actions.

When I arrived at my hotel, Nolan was standing outside my room door. He appeared to be relieved that I was there instead of at home with my husband.

"I see you made the right decision."

"I don't want to talk, Nolan."

"I was just making sure you're okay."

"I'm okay. You can go," I said as I unlocked the door and walked into the room.

"Why are you so angry at me?" he asked as he followed behind me. "All I ever did was make sure you had everything you needed, gave up months of my life and all of my savings so you and my cheating brother could have a baby. Now, *I'm* the bad guy?"

"Don't keep reminding me what you gave up. You act like I'm not thankful for everything you did. I just think it's a bad idea for us to meet like this."

"Why? Because I make you feel good? Because you can't control yourself around me?"

"Nolan, I—" he stopped me with a kiss. I broke away from him. "I need some time."

"How much?"

"I don't know. A few days."

"Okay," he said reluctantly. "I'll call you in the morning."

I nodded, walked him to the door, closed it, locked it, and leaned against it. I thought about the story my mother-in-law told me when I first married Dolan. She said running might be the easiest thing to do, but not always the smartest. I wanted to cry because I honestly didn't know what to do. I also didn't know what I got myself into, but I damn sure wanted out.

I left the hotel and called Nuni. He knew something was wrong the moment he heard my voice. He convinced me to come out to Nebraska to spend some time with him. When I arrived, he made sure I had a safe place to stay, and once I settled in, he pounced on me. I tried to play it off, but he wasn't having it.

"Okay, girlfriend, you stalled long enough. Gon' ahead and spill that tea."

"Well, we couldn't get pregnant so . . ."

"Yes?"

"We went to a sperm bank and . . ."

"Chile, if you don't stop beating around the bush."

"Dolan's brother ended up being our donor and . . ."

"Dolan's fine-ass brother, Greg?"

"Hell no."

"Nolan?"

"Yes."

"I knew there was something different about you, girl-friend. Are you preggo?"

"I'm not sure."

"Honey, what are you doing here? You need to be home decorating your nursery."

"When the procedure didn't work, I ended up staying at Nolan's. I'm here because Dolan cheated."

"Before or after you started sleeping with your brother-in-law?"

I was speechless.

"Girl, you need to talk faster. The suspense is killing me."

I filled him in on the drama that was happening in my life as best I could. I didn't go into all the details but based on what I told him, he understood my current dilemma and agreed to support my decision to stay away from both men.

I cut and dyed my hair, got colored contacts, and changed the way I dressed. I kept to myself and only associated with one other person, Ari, a woman who lived in my apartment building. Ari was a good cook and often brought food for me to eat. She also kept me company while Nuni was at work.

Today made a month since I left behind everyone I knew and loved. Everyone except Nuni, that was. While he did everything he could, including letting me drive his car and securing an apartment for me to make me comfortable in my new surroundings, it was nothing like home.

I was feeling out of sorts and decided to see a doctor. Based on my symptoms of nausea, tender breasts, and a missed period, I knew I had to see an OB/GYN. The office was crowded that day, and I wanted nothing more than to go back home and climb in bed. But I had put it off for three days and didn't want to wait any longer.

I filled out the paperwork with my maiden name, Ross, pulled out my cell phone, and prepared for the long wait to see the doctor. Fifteen minutes later, the nurse called me in to check my vitals and had me put a urine sample in a cup, then sent me right back into the crowded waiting room.

Thirty minutes later, she called me into the room where I waited another ten minutes to see the doctor. He came in, introduced himself, and got right to the heart of the matter.

"Congratulations, Mrs. Ross. You're pregnant." I gave him a horrified look.

"Are you okay, ma'am?" he asked.

"I'm fine," I whispered almost inaudibly.

"You seem disappointed. Is there anything I can get for you, some water or something?"

"No, thank you." I smiled. It was the first one the doctor saw on my face since I arrived.

"Most of the girls that come to this clinic are young, inexperienced, and not at all happy about being pregnant, but the married ones are jumping up and down. I thought you'd be ecstatic."

"I'm fine."

"Here's your prescription for prenatal vitamins. Please see my receptionist for your next appointment. I'll see you next time," he said as he handed me the papers like I ruined his day.

"Thank you."

I went to the receptionist's desk, got my appointment, and headed to the pharmacy to pick up my prescription. The old lady sitting in the seat by the door looked out of place in an office full of pregnant women, but I'd seen odder things.

The cold wind made me shiver as I walked to my car on the far side of the parking lot. I shuffled along in a state of shock as the news of my pregnancy loomed over me. A few months ago, I would have been ecstatic about having a baby, but now, I wasn't so sure. The move to another state seemed to bring me a new purpose, and I was beginning to adjust to my new life. Now, I had to figure out what I was going to do.

It wasn't like I was without talent. I knew I could get a good recommendation for a job as an elementary school teacher. I was also an excellent interior decorator and had already set my sights on some new clientele. I wasn't planning on being a single parent, but it was definitely something I would have to consider.

I had imagined my first pregnancy to be an exciting moment where I would gather the people I loved and announce the good news. But now, I was ashamed and uncertain of my baby's and my future. There would be no champagne toasts or celebrations at a restaurant. As a matter of fact, I couldn't think of anyone I wanted to tell.

Nolan and Dolan had called me several times, but I changed phones awhile back. The only time I checked the old one was to get my messages. I only gave my new number to April, Mama, and Nuni because I knew they wouldn't share it with anyone.

I still couldn't understand why Dolan slept with a woman that everyone called a slut at the mention of her name. She was one of his ex-girlfriends whom he left because she slept with several people he knew, and he'd known her since junior high school. Yet, he chose to keep that piece of information from me too. Since Dolan didn't like condoms, I knew he didn't use one with that hooker. So, needless to say, our marriage was a wrap.

Nolan was another story. He started out great in the beginning, and I grew to love him as a friend, but he went over the deep end after we slept together and actually thought it was a good idea for us to be together. If I chose to leave my husband, it wouldn't be for him. To top it off, his crazy ex-girlfriend was showing up everywhere I went. If I didn't know any better, I would say the woman was a certified stalker.

Dolan

I woke up bright and early and felt for my wife. Every day I wished she was by my side, and that it was a nightmare she wasn't with me. I drove up to the precinct for the thirtieth time, determined to get some answers.

"Any word on my wife yet?"

"No, Mr. Rogiers. We don't have any leads," the detective answered.

"It's been a month since I filed the missing person's report. You guys should have something by now."

"I know how long it's been. You come in here every day."

"And I will continue to do so until you find my wife."

"You told us yourself your wife left because she thought you cheated on her. It looks like she just up and left you. You might just need to accept that."

"Don't tell me to accept it. Nobody's seen her in a month. My wife wouldn't just up and leave. I think something happened to her."

"In my professional opinion, Mr. Rogiers, your wife moved on with her life. Some women don't play when you cheat."

"I think you need to do your job and look harder for her. I'll be watching, so you better not leave any stone unturned." I stormed out of the precinct mad as hell. I'd gone without my wife for so long that I was beginning to think I lost my mind. I'd been drinking so much, I couldn't even function at my job. I knew people smelled the liquor on my breath, but I didn't care.

Miko had shown up a few times at my house, and I almost beat the shit out of her. I don't think she'd ever seen me that mad, but I really turned the tables on her ass.

Miko

Dolan pushed me so hard on the ground my adrenaline started pumping like crazy. I was waiting for him to rip my clothes off and make mad love to me on the spot, like most of the men in my life, but he looked at me like I was a piece of scum and refused to let me touch him. He threatened to ban me from him forever if I didn't tell him everything I knew. I didn't want to lose him, so I agreed to tell him the truth. My story made his skin crawl.

"On the night you agreed to come to my house and talk, I called Darica's number from your phone. I waited until she answered the phone; then I pulled out your dick and started sucking like crazy. You remember that, don't you, daddy?" Dolan didn't say anything. He just motioned for me to continue.

"I disconnected the call right before you pushed me away. Darica must have heard everything and assumed you cheated." I looked over at Dolan like I did something cute. I knew he wanted to beat me for causing him to lose his wife, and I would have accepted that. I needed something from him, even if it was physical pain. Even I knew cheating was the one thing Darica didn't tolerate, and I had caused Dolan to go over the deep end. As much as I wanted him, I knew he wouldn't be able to rest until he found her and made everything right between them.

Dolan

I felt Nolan knew something about the incident with Miko and me because he scowled at me like I committed a cardinal sin. He was the last person who could judge me when it was obvious he fucked multiple women for sport. What kind of brother sides with the sister-in-law? I knew I would find out the answer to that question soon enough. The only thing I wanted to focus on now was finding my wife, even if I had to do it myself.

Nolan

Even with a private investigator, I couldn't locate Darica, and I thought I was going to lose my mind. Litha Jones came highly recommended and was supposed to be the best in the business.

"My work is guaranteed," she told me. "But I have to tell you, I have my work cut out for me. Darica didn't leave much of a trail. She checked out of that hotel in the wee hours of the morning, and her credit card hadn't been used since that day almost a month ago. She withdrew a lot of money from her bank account, closed it, and is possibly paying cash for everything she purchases. No one's seen a woman fitting her description in the vicinity."

"So, how are you going to find her?"

"I'll find her," she assured me. "I have eyes everywhere."

"My connections in the medical industry might be able to help. I think she might be pregnant."

"That information will be helpful," Litha said. "We'll be in touch."

My ringing phone shook me out of my deep thoughts. I looked at the caller ID and cringed.

"What do you want, Evette?"

"Is that any way to talk to your future wife?"

"Say what you have to say before I hang up."

"Baby, this has gone on long enough."

"What?"

"Us being apart."

"What we had is over, Evette."

"What does she have that I don't?"

"Who?"

"Your sister-in-law."

"She's my brother's wife, you idiot."

"I saw the way you looked at her, the way you talked to her. You fucked her, didn't you?"

"You're delusional. Get a life."

"Damn, Nolan. That's messed up."

"What I do is none of your business."

"I don't care what you did. I still love you."

I hung up the phone and poured another glass of Rémy. I didn't have time for Evette's shenanigans.

"I see you're popular with the ladies," the hooker said as she exited the bathroom.

"Did I ask for your opinion?"

"It's all good, baby," she sang. "I know that look anywhere."

"Whatever."

"Is she going to be able to handle your appetite?"

"What?"

"The woman you're in love with."

"What are you still doing here?"

"Making sure you're full."

"I'm fine."

"It didn't help, did it?"

"What?"

"You fucked me three times, but it did absolutely nothing for you."

"Don't worry about it," I said as I paid her and walked her to the door. I was hoping Evette was out there watching. That was the main reason I had her come over. I also thought she could relieve some of my stress, but she was right; it didn't work. I needed Darica. I hadn't been right since the last time I was with her. This proved to me that I would be good, as long as I had the right woman.

I watched television until I fell asleep and woke up a few hours later to my phone ringing off the hook. When I answered, Litha was on the line.

"Where have you been?" she answered frantically.

"What's going on?" I said as I sat up.

"I think I found Darica."

"Oh shit, where?"

"In a small town in Nebraska. The eye color and hair don't match her description, but the height and weight do. One of my associates in a medical clinic called and told me about a woman going by the name of Mrs. Ross. That's her maiden name, right?"

"Yes."

"She came in the clinic for a pregnancy test. She didn't blend in with the rest of the patients."

"Where is she now?"

"I lost her. She caught me trailing her, so I had to stand back."

"What the hell you mean you lost her?"

"Calm down. My associate's going to call her and get her address today."

"Damn. This is crazy."

"I'll let you know when I find out more."

"Okay. Thanks."

Evette

When I saw the hooker-looking bitch that came out of Nolan's house, I wondered how many bitches one man could have. It didn't make any sense for him to be so greedy when all he needed was one woman. She knew I was following her, but I didn't care. I wanted to know what she was doing in there with my man, so I straight out asked her.

"What the fuck were you doing in there?"

"None of your goddamn business," she spat.

"Oh, you're a smart bitch."

"Yeah, and I can back it up. I guess you're supposed to be his wife or something."

"Not yet."

"You mean this nucca got you following him around, and y'all ain't even married?" The bitch laughed.

"Stay away from him, and you won't have a problem."

"The dick was good, but I don't want your sorry-ass man. But I think it's only fair to warn you; I will come back if his price is right. He pays good, and he tips."

"Did he use a condom with you?"

"My time is money, bitch. If you ain't paying, I ain't playing."

I threw the ho a twenty, and she kicked it away from her. I gave her a one-hundred-dollar bill, and she sang like a bird.

"Yeah. He used a condom and pulled out."

"How much will it cost me to get you to forget you ever met him?"

"You can't pay me enough. The dick is good, and he knows how to use it. Truth be told, he was the best I ever had. He practically did all the work. In this business, that doesn't happen every day."

"That was the wrong thing to say," I said as I drove a knife into her back. Lucky for me, it was dark, and we were right next to my car. I dragged her to my trunk, popped it, and hoisted her ass in. I already had it lined with trash bags, but I was hoping the blood wouldn't leak anywhere. Too bad she was such a dummy. I was going to let her live when I saw she wasn't a threat. But bitches needed to watch how they talked about my man. Now, she was one less problem for me to worry about.

I guess something scared Darica away because she left town, and I heard her husband was going out of his mind with worry. I knew she saw me following her, but I didn't care. The way my man was sniffing behind her was pitiful, and I needed to send a message to her that he was off-limits.

Chapter Ten

Darica

I sat quietly in my dark apartment reeling from the news I just received. I'd always imagined that finding out I was pregnant would make me jump up and down, but for some reason, it made me depressed. I couldn't eat and didn't want to sleep. My phone rang, and I didn't want to answer it, but the caller ID showed that it was the clinic, and I didn't want to miss any information they needed to tell me. For all I knew, they were calling to say they made a mistake and the pregnancy test was negative.

"Hello."

"Hello, Mrs. Ross?"

"Yes."

"We forgot to get your address. Can you give us the information for our files?"

"Sure," I said as I gave the young woman an address.

"Thank you," she said.

"You're so welcome."

I was a little disappointed that the receptionist didn't have anything else to tell me, so I turned on the TV and channel surfed to break the silence. I gave up when I found nothing on and took it as a sign that I needed to grab some much-needed rest.

As soon as I got comfortable on the couch, I heard faint knocks at the door. Initially, I wasn't going to answer it. I didn't know too many people here, so the visits were often from people with the wrong address. I tried to lie back down and get some sleep, but the knocks continued, so I got up, looked out of the peephole, and saw that it was Ari holding a plate and a soda in her hands. I didn't feel like company, but I was grateful for the woman. She always extended herself by bringing me food, and I didn't want to leave her outside in the hallway. I unlocked the deadbolt and yanked the door open.

"Aww, honey. You shouldn't have."

"I saw you walk in with nothing, and I knew you didn't cook. I wasn't going to eat without feeding you." She had on a silver bracelet that said, *One in a Lifetime.*

"Thank you. It smells delicious."

"Thanks, I used to date a gourmet chef. He taught me a few tricks."

I took the foil off the plate and brought it to the microwave to heat up.

"This food is still hot."

"Yes. I just finished cooking."

"So, you didn't eat either?"

"No, I wanted to make sure you had a hot meal first. Enjoy."

"Wait. I don't want to eat alone."

"Say no more. Let me grab my plate and my cell phone, and I'll be right back," she said.

Ari came back five minutes later with a bottle of wine. I set the table and got out some wineglasses.

"So, how did your visit go?"

"What visit?"

"Your doctor's visit."

"Oh, it went well. I'm fine."

"Do you have any family?" she asked. There was a pregnant pause, and Ari instantly looked embarrassed. I guess she felt like she was prying in my business. "I'm sorry. I shouldn't have asked that. If you wanted me to know, you would have volunteered it."

"It's okay. I just had a moment. I have a mother and a husband. But we're about to get divorced, though."

"Oh, I'm so sorry."

"Don't be. It's complicated."

"So, are you planning to settle down here in Nebraska?"

"I don't know, but I'm sure I'll figure it out soon enough. I like it here."

"I love the way you decorated this place. Is that your profession?"

"Actually, I'm a schoolteacher, an art schoolteacher."

"Same thing. You have a flair for creativity."

"What do you do?"

"I'm just a stay-at-home person on disability," Ari said apologetically. "It is what it is."

"Not judging." I poured more wine into our glasses.

Ari gulped hers down and poured another. We sat in silence as we ate our food. Eventually, the effects of the alcohol worked its magic on Ari, who loosened up and became talkative.

"I used to be a college student, you know. I was going to school to be a nurse."

"That's a wonderful profession. What made you stop?"

"Typical story; fell in love, got pregnant."

"Really?"

"Yes."

"How old is your baby?"

"Would have been two."

"Would have been?"

"Yes. The child didn't make it."

"Oh, I'm sorry. What happened to your baby daddy?"

"He went over the deep end, got mad, and left."

"You're still young. You can try again."

"I'm over it. What about you? What's your story?"

"Husband cheated, I left. End of story."

"How are you feeling?"

"I feel OK, just a little numb, but I'll be okay. I always bounce back."

"Ain't that the truth? That's the one thing we women do best. Did you have any kids with him?" Ari asked. But before she could get the words out, I got up from the table, ran to the bathroom, and vomited up my dinner. I rinsed my mouth and patted my face with cold water before returning to the kitchen.

"I'm so sorry," Ari apologized. "I hope my food didn't make you sick."

"Of course not. I think I just overindulged. Plus, I normally don't drink wine."

"OK," Ari said with a look of relief. "I guess that's my cue to leave. Thanks for the company."

"Thanks for dinner."

"No problem, love," Ari said as she gathered her dishes and left.

Nolan

I was in a deep sleep when I heard my phone buzzing on the nightstand. When I saw Litha's number show up on the caller ID, I almost broke my neck trying to reach over and answer it.

"Hello."

"Hi, Nolan. I got that information for you."

"Great." I sat up in bed and grabbed a pen off the nightstand. "What is it?"

"She only gave the street number and address."

"It's cool; we can google the city."

"OK. It's 111 Main Circle," she read.

"Oh shit, that's her mother's address."

"Are you serious?"

"Yes. I ride by there every day."

"Damn. The receptionist must've assumed it was a Nebraska address. It's obvious Ms. Darica doesn't want to be found."

"That's for sure."

"I'll stay on it. I'm sure we'll find her soon."

"I hope so," I said as I hit the end button on my phone. I was sick of waiting and knew I had to take matters into my own hands. I searched my contacts for the phone number I needed, the only person who could help me.

Dolan

I decided I wasn't going to keep going to that precinct. Those pricks didn't want to help me, and it was obvious they weren't going to do their job. I started searching for my own clues. People didn't just disappear into thin air. I was sure my wife had to be somewhere she felt comfortable. She wasn't the obvious type, so I knew she wouldn't make it easy for me.

I reached into the closet to look for something that would point me in the right direction. I found pictures and an old cell phone, along with a cord to power it up. I plugged it and flipped through an old photo album while I waited for it to light up.

The pictures dated back three years ago when Darica had her hair in a short pixie cut. She looked so cute in her pink, off the shoulder crop top that showed her pierced belly button. She had on a pair of tight jeans that hugged her curves, and it made me long to be inside her.

The next picture was of her and April. They were dressed like twins with matching Freakum dresses that hugged their perfect curves. Darica's was fuchsia, and April's was orange. In the middle of them was their friend, Nuni. I always wondered whatever happened to him. She used to talk to him a lot, and they all used to hit the club on the weekends, but eventually, it was only Darica and April.

The cell phone buzzed, indicating it was powered up. I turned it on and immediately went to the text messages.

Nuni: Hey, girlfriend, I made it safely to Nebraska.

Darica: I still don't understand why you had to move so far away.

Nuni: It's the new land of opportunity.

Darica: I can't think of any opportunity in Nebraska that would make me go there.

Nuni: I keeps an open mind, baby.

Darica: Well, don't be a stranger.

Nuni: Of course not, bestie. I love you.

Darica: I love you more.

I tried Nuni's number, but it was disconnected. I knew Darica had to have a current number somewhere. I thought about asking April for it, but I knew she was probably angrier at me than Darica was, so she was definitely not going to cooperate. I knew she had Darica's new number and address because Darica didn't make a move without telling her.

I was twirling the cell phone in my hand, and a thought crossed my mind. I was so silly. The answer to all my problems was literally in the palm of my hands. I logged into the cell phone website and pulled up our phone records. The last call Darica made on our old plan was a month ago to a number in Nebraska.

Bingo.

April

I was excited about my unexpected guest. The last time I saw his sexy ass, he was telling me how much he loved another woman. I didn't want to let go, but I believed in love, and anyone who wanted to pursue it was cool with me.

When I heard his sexy baritone on the other side of my door, I couldn't believe my ears. I yanked the door open and almost fainted when his piercing eyes greeted me. His cologne attacked my nostrils and immediately acted as a pheromone, sending my hormones into a frenzy.

"Hey, you," I said as I extended my hand to invite him in. He stepped in and looked around. I had done some redecorating, and my place was winning.

"Hey, yourself," he said.

I was glad I had on my yellow dress, was freshly showered and perfumed, and had completed my look with a pair of Michael Kors sandals that highlighted my bright yellow pedicure. His eyes focused on my perfect C cups that looked even better in a push-up bra.

"To what do I owe this visit?"

"I know it's short notice, but I was wondering if I could use your shower. I just finished a long shift at the hospital, and your house was closer than mine, so I decided to stop. I hope you don't mind," he said.

"Not at all. Make yourself at home."

His bright smile filled the room. "Thanks a bunch, love. I'm not inconveniencing you, am I?"

"No. I wasn't doing anything special," I lied. In truth, I was headed out on a date but decided I'd rather stay home with this fine specimen than meet up with old stuck-up Grant. "Towels are in the closet," I told him as I pointed toward the bathroom.

"Cool," he answered as he made his way down the hall. I wasted no time calling Grant.

"Um, can we take a rain check?"

"Sure," Grant said disappointedly.

"Okay, I'll call you when I'm free."

"I hope you're not having second thoughts about going out with me."

"No, it's not that; it's just something came up."

"Okay, love, just call me when you're ready."

"I sure will," I cut him off. "Thanks. Bye."

Nolan

When I came back down the hallway, April was sitting on the couch looking uncomfortable in her own house.

"Excuse me."

"Yes?" April said as she looked me up and down like I was the sexiest thing she ever laid eyes on in her life. I was standing there dripping wet with nothing but a towel on. My bulging muscles were everywhere, and the imprint of my well-endowed rod was pushing up the towel.

"Goddamn, motherfucker," April mouthed. I laughed as I watched her huge nipples poking at the fabric of the flimsy dress.

"Can you do me a favor?"

"If it includes squirting," she said as she covered her mouth with her hand. "I'm sorry, but you look like a page right out of Pornhub. What did you need?"

"Just my duffle bag," I said, pointing to the couch. "It has my clothes in it."

"Okay," she said as she handed it to me.

"Thank you."

"You're welcome."

"April?" I asked.

"Yes."

"What's Pornhub?" I winked as I disappeared down the hall. I quickly dressed in jeans and a T-shirt, but that didn't stop anything. April had seen my perfect body, and that image would forever remain etched in her memory. I laughed as I walked into the living room to execute the rest of my plan.

Dolan

I walked out of the Nebraska airport with a spring in my step. I didn't have to go to baggage claim because I packed light. I wouldn't be here long because I only had one goal, and that was to bring my wife home safely.

Darica had truly fucked up. Not only did she go to Nebraska, but she went to Aurora, a small town where one of her best friends lived, and he had a rather unusual name. I could literally knock on every door and run into her by nightfall or look in the phone book and find him instantly. Decisions, decisions.

What Darica didn't understand was that I played for keeps, and I was not going to let something this small break up our marriage. I already dealt with Miko about what she did, and I got her ass so straight, it would take ten men to bend her back. I knew she would think twice before she jeopardized my marriage again.

I couldn't have my wife on the other side of the world when we were supposed to be building our future together. So what if we were doing it with somebody else's seed. If my brother didn't like the way things were going, we would just pick a donor off the clinic's list. His shit wasn't working for us anyway. Maybe he was shooting a couple of blanks of his own. It shouldn't take this long to make a baby by artificial insemination.

I stepped out onto the sidewalk, grabbed the first taxi I saw, gave the driver the hotel address, and relaxed my eyes while I listened to my Tupac CD.

Nolan

I teased April with my tongue, twirling it in her mouth like I was trying to touch her tonsils with it, while I palmed her left breast with my right hand. She was moaning and fondling my erect manhood with her left hand, acting like she was about to die if I didn't fuck her now.

I pushed her dress up around her waist and her panties to the side. I didn't want to have sex with her, but I had to do something to make her happy so she would let her guard down. I was thinking about tasting her because that alone would've made her give up the information I needed. I knew she would love that because she was always talking about it. But the last thing I needed was for her to run to Darica to tell her how heavenly my tongue felt.

Her phone rang, and I noticed she had her eyes closed, ignoring it. It was obvious she felt nothing was more important than fucking me. I strained to see who was calling her. The phone lit up a number with no name by it.

Her doorbell rang, and her eyes immediately flew open. Instantly, she came out of her Nolan-induced stupor to look at the door.

"Aren't you going to answer that?" I asked.

She got up to answer the door, and I heard a male voice say, "I know you heard me calling your phone, April." That let me know that the person calling was the same person at the door.

As they were arguing about her standing him up, I picked up her phone. She didn't have a lock on it, so I scrolled down and checked her logs. I found a person she had named as Bestie, wrote down the number, put her phone back on the table, and headed to her rescue. It was the least I could do since I used her to get to the woman of my dreams.

A fool named Grant wanted to fight over April.

"Look, man, April and I are just friends," I explained.

"You need to leave," April told him. She obviously wanted to get back to business.

"You know how much I want to be with you, April. I know you cancelled on me because of him. How could you do this to me?"

April was trying to shut her door on him, but he had his foot in it.

"You're just making the situation worse," I told him.

"I agree. I'm sorry, April," he said as he walked to his car in defeat.

April was livid as she walked back into the living room with me. She was visibly shaken.

"If you feel unsafe, I can rent you a room for the night."

"That won't be necessary," she sighed.

I felt sorry for her, but I desperately needed to get in touch with Darica.

"At least let me take you to your mother's house. Promise me you'll stay the night."

"OK," she nodded.

I dropped her off and immediately went home and studied the phone number. I googled the area code and found out it was a Nebraska phone number that was difficult to trace because it was a cell phone. I booked a flight right away.

After what seemed like forever, my plane touched down in Nebraska. I was so anxious to see Darica, but I realized I had my work cut out for me. According to Litha, she had to get ahold of her friend that tapped into cell phone databases. He was on vacation, and it would take awhile for her to reach him because he was on an island and still had to get in touch with his contact in the States.

After I checked into my hotel room at the Marriot, I lay on the bed to relax while I waited for the information. I looked at the phone number once again and wondered if it really belonged to Darica. I played around with the number for a while, then dialed it from my burner phone. Sure enough, she answered. Her voice sounded so good, I almost called out to her, but I realized how stupid that would be. I hung up the phone, glad that I at least got a chance to hear her voice.

I wished I had enough influence to convince her to come home, but I was the very thing that forced her to run. I thought about how cool it would be if I got her pregnant and how much I would love to hold her and help her through her pregnancy.

My phone rang. I snatched it up and answered without bothering to see who it was.

Dolan

After checking into the hotel, I took a quick nap, freshened up, and took a taxi to Enterprise Rental. The two-hour wait was ridiculous but well worth it when I drove away with the family car I wanted, a blue Honda Accord that would allow me to blend in if I needed to. Lucky for me, Nuni was listed in the phone book, and his house was only a few miles from the rental company. I punched in the address on my GPS and took the seven-mile drive over there. I wasn't sure what I would say to him because I knew Darica had already told him the story of how I cheated.

I still couldn't believe how one drink had led to all this drama. I only went to Massey's that day to have a gin and tonic to take the edge off, but Miko had to bring her ass in there and fuck up everything. My mother always told me never to put my hands on a woman. But she didn't say anything about paying some women to do it for me. After she ran into the crew I sent to *talk* to her, she agreed to help me, and I knew she would most definitely think twice before she messed with my family again. My dumb ass should've seen it coming, though. Miko had never been any good, and trying to be her friend was a big mistake that cost a lot.

I knew my wife loved me, and if I could get her to sit still long enough to listen to what I had to say, I knew she would come home with me.

"Damn," I said as I hit the steering wheel. Nuni's house was in a gated community like all the houses in this area. Now, I had to find a way to get into this place. It was only three o'clock. I should have thought about the fact that Nuni might be at work. I decided to wait until I saw him come in the gate.

Nolan

"What's up?"

"Hey, baby," Mina blurted. "I been looking all over for you. I called you like a million times. Why aren't you answering my calls?"

"I was busy," I answered coldly.

"Okay. Do you want to grab something to eat and meet me at my place?"

"I'm out of town."

"Okay. Hit me up when you get back, daddy. I really miss your loving."

"Mina, I've moved on."

"Okay. I don't mind coming to see you wherever you live."

"I didn't move on to *somewhere* else. I moved on to someone else."

"You mean like a new chick?"

"I mean like a new woman," I mocked her.

"I don't know what to say, Nolan. I'm so in love with you," she cried.

"I'm sorry, but it's for the best. I'm sure you'll find someone that's compatible with you."

"He won't be like you. You are everything. Please don't leave me, Nolan."

"I have to go," I said unsympathetically as I hung up.

My phone rang as soon as I hung up, and I almost didn't answer because I thought it was Mina calling to harass me again. But when I looked at the caller ID and saw that it was Litha, I answered the phone with a quickness.

"Hey."

"Guess what?" she said.

"What's up?"

"We found her."

I was so relieved that I could barely speak. "Where is she?"

"She's about a block away from you."

"Oh my God. She's been right down the street from me the whole time?"

"Yes, sir. You ready for this address."

"I stay ready."

Chapter Eleven

Darica

"Don't move," Ari said as she glided the blade across my eyebrows. She was wearing a bracelet that said, "*Never Meant 2 Hurt U.*"

I'd never had my eyebrows done, and it was scary, wondering if she was going to cut me.

"All done, scaredy-cat," she teased.

I ran to look in the mirror and saw she did a wonderful job. The shape of my eyebrows gave my face an entirely different look.

"You are so talented," I complimented her.

"It's nothing."

"Yes, it is. You sew, you do hair and makeup, and you make bracelets."

"I have them made."

"But you come up with the quotes."

"I get the idea from songs. I believe there's a song for every situation."

I suddenly thought of the song game. "I guess a lot of folks believe in that," I said. "I kept up my end of the deal. Now, it's your turn."

Earlier today, she was crying her eyes out about the child she lost and the man she lost right along with it. It made me depressed. Maybe it was because I knew how it felt to want a child. I promised her I would let her do my eyebrows if she told me the details. I wanted to give her a chance to vent because I doubted that she ever told anyone her story. She took me up on my offer.

"It all started when I was struggling to pay my college tuition," Ari began. "I worked two or three jobs, but it was all for nothing. My check was so short that paying the rent was a challenge, let alone school expenses, bills, and utilities.

"Someone told me about donating my eggs. At first, I thought it was pretty horrific to take money for something so sacred, but when I read the brochure and saw that many women did it, I felt a little bit better. I went to the classes where they explained the process of helping someone who couldn't have children. Next thing I knew, I was filling out the questionnaire and talking to a counselor.

"A few weeks later, I was approached by a man. He was extremely handsome and made small talk with me. At first, I thought he was trying to come on to me, but he remained friendly. After about a week of talking to him, he propositioned me.

"'Me and my wife can't have babies, and we need your help,' he said.

"'You have to go through the clinic,' I told him.

"He said, 'If you help us, I'll pay you more than the clinic would ever think about giving you.'"

"I eyed him suspiciously, wondering if this was a setup the clinic came up with to catch unsavory participants. I didn't want to get disqualified before I had a chance to make any money. 'What's the catch?' I asked.

"Instead of getting your eggs from the clinic, me and my wife would use your body to carry the child to term; then when you have the baby, it would belong to us."

"So, you want me to carry a baby for you with your seed?"

"'Yes,' he said, looking annoyed that I would say something so stupid. 'Whose seed did you think we were going to use? Your boyfriend's?'

"'No, sir,' I shook my head. 'I don't have a man right now.'

"This guy was fine as hell. I could see why his woman wanted to have his baby."

"'Let me think about it,' I told him.

"'You have one day,' he warned.

"The first thing I thought was this motherfucker has a lot of nerve approaching me to ask if I would have a baby for them, then gives me a deadline. I had to admit he was paying well, and he was so fine I would probably have had his baby for free. I agreed to their terms. We tried the turkey baster method, but it didn't work.

"I'm going to have to have sex with you the natural way, but don't get it twisted. This is not a come-on. I love my wife, and I just want to give her a baby."

"I understand," I told him.

"The day he came over, I was past excited. I hadn't been with a man for six months, and the thought of being with him made me weak. He was handsome, sexy, and intelligent. I was dying to have a child with him, even if I was going to be giving it away to him and his wife.

"He came over with champagne, chocolates, strawberries, and roses, cooked for me, fed me the chocolates and strawberries dipped in whipped cream, and gave me sips of champagne. I was like, damn. I'd never had a man like him. Where do they do that at, where did he come from, and how do I find more like him?

"When he laid me down, I was more than ready. His dick was the most beautiful thing I had ever seen in my life. Yes, I'm a size queen, and he was perfect for me, but I didn't expect him to be so well endowed.

"If I thought that was surprising, his sex game was on point. He had me bent over the bed froggy style, doggie style, and in every position imaginable. I was like, damn, I thought I was just going to get missionary. But this man right here was the truth. He made me come so many times that I lost count.

"I was a little sad when it was over . . . until he said those magic words that made my heart race."

"We need to do this every day you're ovulating. That way, we can be sure you get pregnant."

"Of course," I said.

"Whenever he came over, I made sure that I was looking good. I changed my hair, the color of my nails and toes, and got me a facial. He was so romantic and beautiful, and his conversations were always on point. He made sure he struck up a decent subject, spoke directly to me, fed me, and gave me liquor to loosen me up before we made love. By the time he was done with me, I was hopelessly in love.

"I took a home pregnancy test when I thought I was pregnant, and one day a few months later, it came back positive, but he also went to the doctor with me to confirm it. His wanted to tell his wife so that she could come with us to the doctor's appointments, but I told him I didn't feel comfortable with her being there. I didn't want that bitch following us. It wasn't about her. She hadn't participated in the act, and she couldn't have babies for him, so why the hell did she think she was entitled to come with us anywhere?

"Besides, he would always take me to lunch, sometimes dinner, and spend time with me after each appointment, and I didn't want her ruining that. By the time I was four months pregnant, I was planning our lives together, and I was pretty sure that he felt the same way about me. How could he not? He was spending almost every waking moment with me, and I was carrying his seed. He even had sex with me, although I had to beg him sometimes.

"All that was left to do was tell his wife. I knew he wasn't going to have the guts enough to do it, but if we were going to be happy, she needed to know. I was going to call and tell her but decided against it—something like this needed to be done in person. I knew where they lived because I had followed him home a few times, just to see how they were living. That condo overlooking the beach was everything, and I could tell he had done everything in his power to provide her a fancy life. I didn't trip because the life we were going to have was going to be even better. All I had to do was show up to speed up the process.

"I rented a car for the occasion, something big enough so that my man could ride home with me with some of his belongings if he wanted to, and I was knocking on their door by noon.

"She answered the door. I wasn't expecting someone so beautiful, but I knew she wouldn't be with him when I was done showing out, so I told myself it didn't matter."

"'Can I help you?' she asked.

"Yes, you can. I'm the woman that your husband is in love with."

"'What am I supposed to do about that?' she said as if it wasn't surprising that a woman was at her door claiming to be with her man.

"We're having a baby together, so I'm going to need you to get out of our way."

"'Do you know how fine my man is, and how many women have tried that?' she barked.

"I pulled out my cell phone and showed her the video of him making love to me, and she gasped and held her stomach as she grasped the full realization of what was going on. Her mouth fell open so wide I thought it was going to hit the ground. She put her hand to her mouth like she was going to throw up and ran like she needed to get to the bathroom. Mission accomplished."

Ari stopped long enough to check my reaction. She could tell I was really tripped out from what she was telling me.

"Wow," I said. "This, I wasn't expecting. If anyone had told me that you were going to say all that, I wouldn't have believed them. You don't seem at all like that type of person."

"Call it a bad case of temporary insanity. I realize now that I was delusional. Don't ever believe any woman that tells you that dick can't change them."

"I won't now. So, whatever happened?" I asked.

"You'll have to wait for the next part," she warned.

"Damn. I was hoping to hear the rest of it now," I said.

"You will soon enough. But after all that talking I just did, I'm hungry and thirsty. Aren't you?"

"I sure am."

"Let's take a break, then. I want to go home and check my cell phone messages. Can you go out to grab some food and wine?"

"Sure," I answered reluctantly, even though I was dying to hear the rest of her story, which, by the way, sounded strangely familiar. I decided to go to a local barbecue spot that I saw in the strip mall not too far from our apartment complex. I heard the food was good, and it always smelled delicious.

I rushed into Lloyds Barbecue, and by the time I made it up to the counter and placed our order, I was so hungry, I couldn't stand myself. This pregnancy was definitely changing my appetite. I'd been eating like a pig.

It took them thirty minutes to finish the order, and when they handed it to me, I almost tore into the food instead of taking it home. I felt bad because I knew Ari was hungry as hell, and I was anxious to get back to hear the rest of that juicy story.

I tried to start my car, but it didn't crank up. I tried it about five times, and nothing happened. Then I realized I forgot to turn my lights off. I thought about calling Ari and asking her to get me, then immediately felt guilty and called Nuni. He would probably curse me out because right about now, he would be getting home from work and wouldn't be happy about having to turn back around and go out again.

Nuni answered the phone with a tired, "Hello," and I felt bad about what I was about to ask him to do after he worked a twelve-hour shift.

"Hey, Nuni."

"Hey, love, how's it going?"

"Not too good. I need a jump."

"What?"

"Sorry."

"Where are you?"

"At Lloyd's Barbecue Plaza."

"I'm on my way," he sighed.

Nolan

It took less than twenty minutes for me to drive to her apartment from my hotel. For some reason, I was nervous about seeing Darica for the first time in a month. I envisioned myself holding her in my arms and telling her how much I missed her and her telling me she missed me just as much. I imagined a pregnant glow on her face and the weight she picked up in all the right places.

I climbed the staircase two steps at a time and paused when I saw a familiar face. At first glance, I thought my eyes were playing tricks on me. I hadn't seen her in years, and I never thought I would again. The last time we were face-to-face, I did some pretty unsavory things. Some I was not proud of, and some I damn near wanted to kick myself for doing.

She caused a lot of pain for me, but I knew I was to blame for much of it. If I had it to do it again, I would definitely do it differently. The surprising part of it all was I never saw it coming. I was so in love with Sheila that I totally disregarded the fact that I was hurting her. I had no intention of making Ari fall in love with me, and I didn't expect to lose a loved one as a result of it.

Ari was coming out of Darica's apartment, which let me know that they had met. If she told Darica anything, it could seriously affect everything I worked hard for. I ran to catch her door before she closed it and forced my way in.

Ari tried to close it on me but was too weak to keep me out. She ran into her room, and I busted down the door. She ran into a closet and locked herself in. I didn't want to make too much noise because I didn't want her neighbors calling the police on me. I didn't come here for that. I came here to bring back the woman I loved. It had taken me years to open up to anyone the way I had opened up to Darica. I wasn't proud of the fact it was her. She was forbidden fruit, bound to a man whose blood ran through my veins. But I was glad I was able to find love again.

Ari was whimpering in the closet as I banged on the door.

"Go away."

"Open the door, Ari."

"I'm sorry about what I did to you. Please don't hurt me again."

She was referring to the day I came over and choked her, but I caught myself and left when I realized it took both of us to create the mess, and I couldn't blame her for all of it.

"Come out. I promise not to touch you."

She slowly opened the door, peeked out, and allowed herself to come out of the closet. Then, she motioned for me to sit in the chair next to her bed.

"I guess you came to finish me off, huh?"

"If I wanted to do that, I would have done it years ago."

"You might as well. I lost the only thing that meant something to me in this world."

"I heard you lost the baby. I'm so sorry."

"Sorry won't bring my baby back."

"I'm confused."

"So, you're just going to act like you didn't have a hand in making me lose it?"

"That's insane. It was my baby too."

"Unbelievable. I guess we're even. I took Sheila from you, so you took my baby from me. We had no right to play God."

"I didn't take anything from you. I thought you had a miscarriage."

"Somebody beat me up. That's how I lost the baby."

"I hope they found the folks who assaulted you."

"No." She shook her head.

"I'm sorry."

"So am I."

"Don't beat yourself up, Ari. Sheila didn't have to kill herself. She had a choice. You shouldn't have confronted her, but what she did had nothing to do with you. I forgive you. I just wish I could forgive myself."

"So you're not here to kill me?"

"No. But I do need to ask you a favor."

"OK."

"The lady that lives across from you, do you know her?"

"Yes."

"Did you tell her about us?"

"I told her about meeting you and about getting pregnant and losing my baby, but she doesn't know it was yours."

"Good. Don't say anything, please."

"Why?"

"It's complicated. I need to be able to tell her myself."

"That's a deal."

"Thank you."

I headed out to see Darica, but when I knocked on her door, Ari told me she went out to get food. For some reason, I didn't feel comfortable waiting for her. I headed back to my hotel disappointed.

Dolan

I watched Nuni pull into the gates and followed him. He was speeding and stopped in front of his house, got out of the car, and headed up the walkway. He got all the way to the door, took a call from his cell phone, then got right back in the car and drove away. I followed him, hoping he would lead me to Darica.

He drove about two miles down the road into a strip mall, got out, and walked to a car where a woman was waiting. I got out my binoculars and zoomed in on Darica.

I ran out of my car, not even bothering to drive the ten rows over. Darica was so surprised to see me; she looked like she was about to faint.

"Hey, baby."

"Dolan . . . What are you doing here?"

"I came to get you. I refuse to live without you."

"Please leave."

"I know you think I cheated and lied to you, but I'm prepared to prove that I didn't. Just hear me out."

Darica didn't say anything, so I facetimed Miko.

"Miko, tell Darica what you told me."

"Darica, Dolan didn't cheat. I orchestrated the whole thing. I called you and staged it."

Darica seemed skeptical until Nuni stepped in.

"Girlfriend, I don't know of any bitch that would help a man get back with his woman after she slept with him, so I'm pretty sure she lied in the first place. Give this man another chance."

"Listen to your friend, baby. I love you and would never cheat on you. I was just in the wrong place at the wrong time. Please take me back, and I will never do it again."

I saw Darica smile for the first time in months. She pulled me in for a hug, and I was ecstatic.

"Okay," she said.

"Can we go home now? I miss you."

"Yes. Just let me pack my things and say goodbye to my friend, Ari."

"'Okay. I'll follow you," I sighed as I made my way to my car.

"Can you give me a jump first?" she smiled.

I felt like a kid in a candy store. I had gone on a mission to bring my wife home and did just that. I was never letting her out of my sight again. I followed Darica to her apartment complex, and she introduced me to her friend, Ari.

Darica had quite a nice setup in the place. It looked so homey; I had to wonder if she missed her true calling. I also wondered if she had entertained any men in it and got jealous at the thought. I looked over at Nuni, who looked equally impressed at the décor.

"Hey, Nuni, I want to thank you for taking such good care of my wife. This is never going to happen again, but it's good to know she was in good hands," I said as I gave him a look that said, "Don't ever do this again without consulting me."

"I got you," he answered. "I hope to find the love that you two have someday."

"You will," I told him as I looked at my beautiful wife. She was packing up a few things in a suitcase, but most of the things she was leaving behind. "You about ready?" I asked her.

"Yes. Let me say goodbye to Ari," Darica said as Ari walked in on cue, and they hugged.

"I am going to miss you so much," she told Darica.

"We'll keep in touch, and I'll be coming out here to see you. I hope you'll visit me too."

"Of course."

"I can't wait to hear the rest of that story, girl," Darica added.

"And I can't wait to tell you," Ari said.

"Keep what you want and donate the rest, okay?" I told her, not wanting to have any reminders that Darica left me and got her own place. "She won't be needing it where she's going."

"You have a lot of nice things here, Darica. Are you sure you want to part with them?"

"I'm positive."

"Okay."

Darica hugged Nuni. "Thank you, my love."

"My pleasure, sweetie. I'm riding with you to the airport if you don't mind."

"Okay," Darica said with a smile.

I escorted my wife into the rental, and we made our way to the airport. The trip was a silent one. I really didn't know what to say to her. It seemed like ages since I'd been with her, and she felt like a stranger, looked like she had undergone some changes, and seemed to have been through a lot in the small amount of time she was away.

I picked up her hand and held it until we arrived at our destination. She still had her wedding ring on, and I smiled . . . until I saw her fingers were swollen. I surveyed her beautiful body and noticed she picked up weight, in all the right places, of course.

Nolan

I went back to Darica's apartment, only to find out she had moved out. Ari told me she left with two men whose names she didn't know. She described them both as handsome and well dressed.

"The tall one sort of reminds me of you, and the shorter of the two would be an excellent catch if he weren't gay."

At first, I couldn't imagine who the hell she was talking about, or why Darica would leave with, not one, but two men. I asked Ari if she would do me a favor.

"Call Darica and tell her she left something, so you can find out who she's with."

"She left everything. Said she wouldn't need it where she was going. They paid me to clean the place, said I could take what I wanted and donate the rest."

"Shit. I hope she's not going home with him."

"Who?"

"Never mind. Just take down my number."

"You got it bad, huh?"

I gave her a look that made the smirk go off her face. "Here's my number," I spat.

She reached out her hand to take the number; then I ran out of the apartment complex, called a taxi, and got to the airport as fast as I could. I gave him an extra twenty to get there quickly. I was just in time to see Darica hug the short guy. The tall one had his back turned, talking on the phone. Even before he turned around, I knew it was my brother.

"Damn!" I yelled loud enough for a group of people to take notice.

I waited for an opportunity to talk to her, and, sure enough, she headed to the ladies' room. I ran in behind her and caught her just before she walked into the stall.

"Nolan, what the hell!" she shrieked.

"I need to talk to you," I said as I put my hand over her mouth until she nodded in agreement.

"You like meeting in bathrooms, don't you?"

"I can't believe you're going home with that loser," I said, ignoring her sarcastic remark.

"That loser is your brother."

"After the way he treated you?"

"He proved to me he didn't cheat."

"How'd he pull off that miracle?"

"Miko admitted she lied on him."

"You believe that shit?"

"Yes."

"He probably threatened her."

"Well, if he did, it didn't show. I saw the whites of her eyes, and it looked like she was telling the truth."

"He dragged her out here to confess?"

"He facetimed her."

"He could've used a fake website for that."

"She was telling the truth. She didn't want to because of her feelings for him, but I could tell she was honest."

I felt weak and helpless. "Darica, please. You're making a big mistake."

"Nolan, he's my husband *and* your brother; how can that be a mistake?"

"Because I love you and need you so much. Give me a chance to show you."

Darica scowled at me like I had lost my mind, and she was right. But I couldn't help myself. I kissed her, held her until she kissed me back, kissed her until it seemed like an eternity. I wanted her to feel what I felt and come home with *me*. Somehow, I knew she wouldn't.

She pushed me away.

"Get out of here before I pee on you."

I walked out of the stall and allowed her the privacy to use the restroom. I lingered close by, hoping she would change her mind. I needed more.

Two women looked at me like they wanted to kick my ass, and a little girl pointed at her mother. "Why is that man in the ladies' room?"

"He shouldn't be," her mother said.

But I didn't care. I was waiting for Darica, and nothing was going to move me.

She walked out of the stall, washed and dried her hands, looked at me, and told me, "I'm not the one for you."

Then she turned away and walked out of my world, the world I knew I should be sharing with her. I wanted to follow her, but I wasn't ready to let anyone know how I felt about her, and I definitely was not ready to face my brother.

Dolan

She was taking so long in that restroom that I thought I was going to have to go in and pull her out. I breathed a sigh of relief as I watched her walk out. I still couldn't believe I had found her. Love took me clear across the country, and I had accomplished the impossible. I didn't want us to miss our flight because I wanted to have a nice romantic evening with her all to myself.

I had to admit, Miko was a saving grace. I knew how she felt about me, so it had to be difficult for her to confess to Darica that she lied about the whole thing. I hoped she had learned a valuable lesson from this stunt and therapy, and that she would turn over a new leaf. Given the right man, I knew she'd make a good wife. She just needed to let all that other stuff go. There was no reason why she couldn't go down the straight and narrow. I told her we could be friends and nothing else. Whether she got the picture was up to her.

I knew Darica probably wouldn't be up to cooking, so I picked up dinner from SeaBreeze. I knew how much she loved the food at that place and not having to cook and clean up after we ate would give us more time to bond. I was excited about having my wife at home, but I knew I had to step up my game.

My brother was no help at all. I thought we were getting close, but this donor situation showed me there was a bigger wedge between us than I thought. I was hoping he would become the brother that I always wanted him to be, but I saw that was not going to happen anytime soon. I hated to disappoint my wife, but we were going to have to go with a donor from the clinic. Maybe my brother needed some time to himself.

I planned to talk to him and make him understand that going against the family was one thing but doing it over a lie, no less, had to be the lowest. It was a shame I was going to have to Facetime Miko yet again, so that he could see that I was telling the truth. With the reputation he had, you would think he would be the first person to understand that some women would do anything to get a man.

Darica was obviously tired because after she ate the seafood, she was sound asleep before her head even hit the pillow. She had slept most of the plane ride, and now she was snoring again. I was hoping that we could spend her first night back making love, but I totally understood. After all, I had waited this long. I lay down beside her to recharge myself. That little ordeal even had me feeling drained.

I was in la-la land and would've slept for another hour, but I woke up to the smell of cleaning supplies and wondered what the hell was going on. *Someone must have gotten my house mixed up with somebody else's,* I thought because a maid was cleaning up the kitchen when I walked in. I was about to tell her that her services were not needed when I heard Darica throwing up in the bathroom.

"Are you okay, baby?" I asked her.

"Yes. I guess it was something I ate," she said.

"Funny, you never had a reaction to your favorite restaurant before."

"There's a first time for everything, baby," she said.

"I guess so." I nodded. I helped her to her feet, grabbed her hand, and led her back to the bed. Once she was all tucked in, I went back to the kitchen to address the cleaning lady.

"There must be some mistake, ma'am," I told her. "I didn't call anyone to clean my house. How did you get in here?"

"Mr. Nolan arranged it," she said.

"Okay, let me call him," I said as I pushed the button to get my brother on the line. He picked up immediately.

"What's up, bruh?" he greeted.

"Hey, there's a cleaning lady here that says you told her to come."

"Oh yeah. I meant to tell you, but I guess it slipped my mind. I heard Darica was home, so I thought it would be nice to have the place all cleaned up for her."

"Why? The place looks fine."

"As I said," he reiterated, "I thought it would be a nice gift for her."

"I said it's not needed, so I'll have the maid pack it up. Everything looks great as it is. You had no business letting her in our house." I hung up the phone mad as hell. Why did he think it was okay to give my wife a gift, brother-in-law or not? Where do they do that at? Apparently, our mother had told him what a mess the place was in when I was depressed. But he should know I wouldn't bring my wife home to a dump. He acted like she should be rewarded for taking off on me.

Nolan got there in five minutes, paid the maid, and acted like he did nothing wrong. "How's everything going?" he asked.

"I'm just glad to have my wife back home," I smirked.

"I'm sure you are," he gloated. "Hopefully, there won't be another misunderstanding."

"There won't." I eyed him angrily. "By the way, I face-timed Miko, so my wife was clear on what happened. I'm going to do the same thing for you."

"That won't be necessary, bruh. I know how some women do."

I was going to say something sarcastic, but I heard Darica coming down the hallway. She must've heard the commotion because the next thing you know, she was asking, "What's going on?" more to Nolan than to me.

"Hey, stranger." He smiled a little too much for my liking. "I heard you were back, so I thought I would surprise you with cleaning services, but Dolan said the house was perfect. He's right. I should've asked first."

"That was nice," she replied.

Nolan was looking at my wife like she was hiding the passkey to a million-dollar lottery. I had never seen him look at anybody with that type of lust, and I could tell he was hoping for some alone time with her. But that wasn't about to happen, not on my watch.

Darica turned on the TV to break the tension. When she asked if anyone was hungry, we both followed her into the kitchen like little puppies. If he even looked like he was going to follow her to any room in this house, I was going to be right there doing a Bobby Brown, every little step she takes.

Chapter Twelve

Nolan

Damn. Dolan was on Darica's ass so close, it was a wonder she could even walk. I bet every time she went to the bathroom, he was right there sitting on the toilet with her. I'd never seen my brother this insecure, and to be honest, I wouldn't have been surprised if he had a chain sitting next to the bed to attach to her to while he slept. I guess her little disappearance act really had him spooked.

Darica was looking a little tired, but, as usual, she was as beautiful as ever. She glowed and looked like she put on a few pounds. My instincts told me to hold her in my arms, but I could never explain that to my brother, especially since he seemed to be looking for a fight. I was looking for a diversion, an excuse, anything to get me into a room with her alone when fate handled it for me.

Darica grabbed her mouth and dashed for the bathroom just as the doorbell rang. Dolan went to answer it, and I decided to follow her. She was heaving over the toilet. I grabbed her hair to keep it from hanging in her face.

"I'm sorry," she apologized. "It must've been something I ate."

"Do you always have this much trouble keeping your food down?"

"What?"

"Have you been throwing up a lot?"

"No," she snapped like she knew what I was implying. I didn't care.

I helped her to the den, sat her down on the couch, and offered to get her some water. She accepted. Darica was playing with my emotions. I'd been around her long enough to know that, so I decided to call her bluff.

"You should probably take a pregnancy test," I said as I handed her the glass of water. She jerked and almost spilled it on the floor.

"I'm not pregnant, just sick," she spat.

"Yeah, and I'm the Prince of Persia. Don't you think our little bundle of joy deserves a celebration?"

"If there was a bundle, Dolan and I would be happy to announce it."

Okay, Darica. Game on, I said to myself.

"Maybe I should ask him to get you a test."

"Why would you do that? I thought we agreed to tell everybody the treatments worked."

"After your little disappearance act, I forgot all about our little agreement. But if you play your cards right, I won't forget again."

"Is that a threat?"

"No. It's a promise."

"What do you want from me?"

"Respect."

"Okay," she said obediently. "You got it."

"You need to work on that announcement before you start showing," I said. I was feeling myself because I had her right where I wanted her.

"I will."

My heart leaped for joy when she said that because she was pretty much confirming her pregnancy. I wanted to hold her in my arms, but Dolan came back in.

"Sorry. That was one of those kids selling cookies. I can never resist those eyes. I bought four boxes."

"It's okay, honey. I'm tired. I'm going to lie down. Will you excuse me?" Darica asked.

"Sure," we said in unison.

"I have to go anyway," I told them.

"Bye!" Dolan said.

I was sure he was happy I was leaving.

Evette

I told Daddy that Nolan was tripping and that I needed his help getting him back. I felt Daddy understood what I was going through since he lost the love of his life over a stupid and scandalous affair. His agreement to help would be out of empathy, as well as guilt for the illegitimate child that resulted from his foolish mistake.

"Evette, I told you," Daddy yelled through clenched teeth, "that man is not an object for you to manipulate at your will! He has a right to decide who he does and does not want to be with."

I was hoping for a more understanding response, but I knew when my father was fed up with my antics. I had asked him to help me with Nolan so many times that I was beginning to sound like a broken record. This time, I had to force myself to cry, so he would feel sorry for me.

"Don't be mean to me, Daddy," I pouted. "I'm sorry to drag you into this, but of all people, you should understand. It was only a few years ago that you went through the same thing with Mama. You did everything to get her back. I'm just following in your footsteps."

"Evette, it's not the same. I was *married* to your mother for seven years. It's been twenty years since she left me and filed for divorce. I'm still trying to get over our breakup."

"But love doesn't have a boundary. It doesn't care if you're married or single. It feels the same, no matter what the situation. Haven't you ever loved someone so much that the thought of losing them makes you sick?"

"Of course."

"Well, that's how I feel about Nolan."

"Be careful with this man. He hasn't committed to you, and to be perfectly honest, I don't think he even loves you."

"You're wrong, Daddy. He's crazy about me. He wants to be my husband."

"Pumpkin, I'll see what I can do. No promises."

"Thanks, Daddy. I love you."

"I love you more."

I happened to be gnawing on a salad while trying to think of a way to get closer to Nolan, when an old friend of mine, Cee, called with even worse news. What she told me almost made me puke up my lunch.

"Hey, Evette."

"What's good?" I asked.

"You know I work at a clinic, right?"

"Yes."

"Nolan visited it a few times."

"Oh?"

"Well, one day he left his keys and one of his colleagues gave me his address, so I decided to take them to him to save him the trouble of coming all the way back to get them. When I got to his house, I saw a car in the driveway and knocked, but nobody answered. So I opened the door with his key and was looking for a spot to leave it in when I heard noises coming from upstairs. They sounded like they were in pain, and I didn't want to leave until I knew everything was okay. I started making my way up the staircase. When I got to the middle of the hallway, I almost thought the man was raping a woman . . . until

I figured out the noises sounded more like moans of passion.

"Embarrassed that I intruded on their privacy, I turned around to leave, but I heard them screaming out each other's names. He was hitting it so hard that I thought he was going to break her in two. I ran out unnoticed, but, to this day, I can't get the images out of my mind."

"What were the names?" I asked.

"Darica and Nolan," she said apologetically. "I'm so sorry about this, friend."

"It's okay. Thanks, Cee."

"You're welcome, girl. I know you'd do the same for me."

I'm not even sure what I said to her or if I even hung up the phone afterward. All I knew was, I was truly devastated.

I knew I should've trusted my instincts the day I confronted them, and he gave me that bullshit about his sister-in-law being his interior decorator. But Nolan had a way of making me feel foolish for my outbursts. I believed him without a second thought. I should've known that Nolan didn't care if she was his brother's wife. As long as she had a cat between her legs, he was fucking her. But I couldn't blame my baby because that ho made him do it. She probably assaulted his dick like a bomb pop. I didn't care how beautiful it was, she had no right touching it, and I wanted to make her pay for her greed.

You see, the way I worked, I was liable to grab that slut, tie her up, and drop her in the middle of the Pacific Ocean. Then Nolan would recognize exactly what I meant when I said he belonged to me. But I was running out of ways to get rid of these hoes, and I was tired of living my life this way. I got lucky with the pregnant one and the fiancée, but I needed to do something that would show Nolan that I was truly his soul mate.

Ari and Sheila were once the bane of my existence, but I got rid of them in one fell swoop. Sheila was my half sister. She and her slutty mother broke up our happy home when I was just 7 years old, and I never forgave them. Sure, I played the role of the perfect big sister when he introduced her after he and Mama divorced. I even pretended to love her for years, but deep down inside, I hated the ground that bitch walked on.

When I saw her at Daddy's party with Nolan, I set out to take him from her because I knew I could. Even though I didn't know he was sleeping with other women, I was still able to fuck up her and her mother's life the way they fucked up mine and got rid of Ari as a bonus.

I befriended Ari's ass when I saw her shopping for maternity clothes, and I faked like I was looking for something to wear when my man eventually knocked me up. I figured by the next year, we would be having a lavish wedding and starting our family soon after.

On the day Ari decided to confess her love for Nolan to Sheila, I followed her. I stood on the staircase, heard the whole conversation, and laughed until I cried. From my angle, I couldn't see the expression on Sheila's face, but I was almost certain it was a pitiful sight. I ran out of the complex and hid behind a tree so that Ari wouldn't see me on her way out. Once I was sure she was gone, I ran back to see what Sheila was up to. The dummy had left her door open, so I was able to walk right in. She was sitting on her couch crying her eyes out.

"You scared the hell out of me." She jumped when she saw me walk in the door.

"I'm sorry. You look like you lost your best friend."

"Worse. I just found out my fiancé got another woman pregnant."

"You're kidding," I said with the fakest surprised expression I could muster.

"I wish I were," she sniffled. I wanted to tell her so badly that neither she nor the lamebrain that just left was going to get Nolan.

"Good. Now you know how it feels."

She lifted her mascara-smeared face, wiped her red nose, and asked, "What did you say?"

"You heard me right. You and your dog-faced mother ruined my life, and you're finally getting payback."

"We had nothing to do with your parents breaking up."

"The hell you didn't. Your mother planned everything, all the way down to the confrontation and getting pregnant with you."

"Don't say that. We're sisters."

"Your weak ass ain't no sister of mine, and you don't deserve him."

"Who?"

"Nolan."

"What does *he* have to do with this?"

"*I'm* the only woman who can fuck him good enough to keep him. A *real* woman that can give him children."

Sheila looked at me like I was insane, and, to some degree, I was. The thought of having to share Nolan with her another day drove me over the edge. I grabbed the gun out of my purse and pointed it at her.

"You don't have to do this, Evette. We can work it out. We'll find a good therapist and get you some help."

"Looks like *you're* the only one who needs to get fixed. I would have given my man a baby by now." She started heaving, crying uncontrollably, and tears fell freely from her eyes. "Shut up. You're pitiful. Grab that pen and paper so you can write."

"What?"

"Pick up the pen before I shoot you in your good-for-nothing stomach." Sheila picked up the pen and looked up at me.

"Have some mercy, Evette."

"I'm letting you come up with your own suicide letter. That's good enough."

When Sheila was done writing the note, I put the gun in her back and walked her up to the rooftop where I pushed her off. Everyone thought she jumped. Nolan was so devastated that he needed a shoulder to cry on, which I was happy to offer him. I had to wait a few months for him to get over her, but it was well worth it.

I know you're probably thinking that my daddy was crazy for helping me get my sister's man. But nothing could be further from the truth. Daddy had set up a fund for Sheila to receive when she turned 20. The only stipulation was that she couldn't be in a serious relationship or married until after she got it. That way, Daddy could ensure she wouldn't blow her money on some loser she chose because she was too young to make rational decisions, or because she might fall prey to some gigolo who only wanted her money.

Sheila couldn't tell Daddy she was with Nolan for obvious reasons, plus the fact that Nolan worked under Daddy, who had no idea they even knew each other before that party and, even then, they played off the true nature of their relationship.

As for Ari, I had her taken care of by way of a group of girls who were willing to beat her up for cash. They punched and kicked her just enough to hospitalize her, and she lost the baby. When Nolan found out she was responsible for Sheila's death, he wanted nothing more to do with her. I don't think he ever knew that I was related to Sheila because Daddy kept her a secret to many of his friends and colleagues. She was deemed a mystery when Daddy invited her to his birthday party, but no one dared to pry into his business. She was too ashamed to tell Nolan this, though she tried on several occasions.

I had covered all my bases and destiny had done the rest. Now, this Darica bitch thought she could just come and steal my man? She needed to take her big head back to her husband and make it work because she had nothing to come for in my camp. I decided to try a less evasive method to get rid of Miss D. All this violence was taking a toll on me.

Dolan

"It seems like we haven't been here in ages." Darica smiled as I pulled up to my parents' immaculate estate. "It's absolutely breathtaking," she added.

"Yes, it is," I agreed. "I want us to have a home like this one day. I'm working on it right now."

"What are you planning to do?" she asked curiously.

"I'm going to start my own business."

"Really?"

"Yes. I'm finally taking my dad up on his offer to help me."

"That's wonderful. What made you change your mind?"

"The fact that we're trying to have a baby made me put life in perspective."

"I'm so happy for you," she said as the smile suddenly disappeared off her face.

"Be happy for both of us. Whatever I have is yours."

"Thank you, baby," she said as I took her hand and led her up the walkway.

"Surprise!" everyone yelled as we walked in.

"OMG, honey, you didn't have to do this for me."

"Yes, I did. You didn't think I was going to let you spend another birthday without a party, did you?"

"I thought we were just going to go out to dinner, but this is a pleasant surprise," Darica said as she started hugging the fifty or so friends and family that were standing in the huge living room.

Nolan was standing in the cut looking at us like he wanted to kick our asses, but I didn't care. I had planned this event for my wife a long time ago, right down to the eighties and nineties music, and I wanted her to have a good time. He was normally so picky about the parties we gave, but since this one was right up his alley, complete with the formal dress code, champagne, caviar, servants, and valet parking, you would think he'd be in la-la land. Instead, he had an attitude the size of Texas about God knows what and was already getting on my nerves.

One of my wife's favorite songs came on. I grabbed her hand so we could cut a rug. I made sure they kept them coming back-to-back, so we could spend plenty of time on the dance floor. I sent a cue to the DJ to put on the slow jams CD from our wedding reception—the one Nolan barely made it to because he ended up getting so drunk the night before. He didn't make it to the wedding at all. At my bachelor party, he was trying to tell me something, but his words were slurred and jumbled.

"Man . . . sh-e-e . . . was sup . . . suppose . . . to . . . be . . . mine. I saw her . . . first. Rescued her . . . from . . . some fool. Brought her back . . . turned my back . . . you took her."

It didn't dawn on me until after our honeymoon what was going on. Even though I initially chalked it up to some drunken fantasy caused by the liquor, I was eventually able to piece together the fact that he was referring to the club where I met Darica. All I remembered him doing on that night was dealing with some hoochie he had dragged in with him. He couldn't recognize a real woman if she came up and bit him.

I had spotted Darica and sent her a drink, but some ugly bastard came and pulled her to the dance floor before she could get it. I looked for her but figured she went to the ladies' room or something. I had pretty much given up hope of finding her when she flagged me down in the parking lot as we were leaving. She was so thankful for the drink; you would've thought I gave her the key to the city. All it took was one date, and I had her.

When Nolan found out we were getting married, he went on some kind of rampage like a little bitch because he felt he saw her first. Then, he showed up at the reception like everything was cool. If I went for the theory that my charm and personality touched her, she'd still be my wife, and if I believed in that love at first sight mess, I looked so much like Nolan, she would've fallen in love with me anyway. Either way, he would've lost.

I should've known he wasn't over whatever bullshit he had going on in his mind. When I pulled my wife in close for a private dance, I looked over at the angry scowl on my brother's face . . . and I knew I was right.

Nolan

The shit was irking me. Dolan had Darica in a headlock, and he thought he was doing something cute. After all these years, I never could understand how my brother took what he did at the club so lightly. I had only walked away for a few minutes to calm my date down. She was feeling kind of awkward that I darted out on her to help a woman some crater-faced motherfucker was trying to rape. I put her in a cab, and the next thing I knew, Dolan was getting Darica's number in the parking lot, and they ended up dating.

Life had me by the balls for a year, and when I finally got around to meeting my brother's fiancée, I was shocked to see it was Darica. I tried not to let it affect me. But it ate away at me like cancer. She brought out feelings in me that were unnatural. Since day one, I wanted her more than my next breath of air.

Dolan may have convinced Miko to recant her story, but he wasn't fooling me one bit. I bet he didn't tell Darica he was binge drinking again. That twisted fool needed to learn a lesson. What he would soon find out was I wasn't letting any child of mine around that madness.

Since I didn't need that loan for the treatments, I used it to purchase an eight-bedroom, five-bathroom house so that I could take care of my family. Dolan was not the man Darica thought he was, and she needed to wake up and smell the coffee. I knew that baby was mine, and knowing what I knew, there was no way in hell I was going to live apart from them. Call me crazy, but it was everything I'd ever wanted. I just didn't see it at first.

I hoped Darica liked the diamond necklace and the dress I gave her. I knew they would look great on her sexy, very alluring body, and I hoped to see her in it at her birthday party, where she would corner me alone and sing praises and thanks. I had to admit that I went all the way out this time. But I wanted to impress her and let her know that she was on my mind. She didn't wear my gifts, but she had on an equally impressive skintight number that showed her beautiful curves. Damn. If only she knew I was going to be thinking about the way she looked tonight for weeks. She was already all that was on my mind lately.

Why the hell did this thing have to turn out the way it did? I'd never in my life felt so crazy about a woman, and, sadly, I didn't care who she belonged to as long as I could have a part of her. With the way she was carrying on, that baby might be all I would have. For now, I at least had her in my thoughts and my dreams. I just didn't know how long they would hold me.

"Hello, Nolan."

"Hello, Doctor Lane. Good to see you. Do you know my brother or sister-in-law?"

"No, I actually came here to talk to your dad. He has a business proposition for me."

"Wow. That sounds great. Is Evette with you?"

"She was supposed to join me, but I think she found something else to get into."

"OK. Well, enjoy the festivities."

"I will, thank you."

I breathed a sigh of relief that Evette would not be crashing this party, but I looked up and saw someone who could equally ruin my evening.

Dolan

"OMG, Ari. What are you doing here?" Darica asked.

"Your mother-in-law invited me."

"How'd she get your information?"

"I don't know, but I'm glad she did. I've never in my life been to an event like this. Thanks so much," she cooed as she grabbed a glass of champagne off a tray.

"You remember my husband, Dolan, and this is my mother-in-law, Rolanda," Darica said after escorting Ari a few feet over to us.

"Nice to meet you," Ari said excitedly. "Thanks for the invite. You have a lovely home."

"Thanks, my love. It's great to meet you too."

"Good to see you again, Dolan."

"Same here, Ari."

"Excuse me. I need to find Millie. I'm almost willing to bet she's in the kitchen harassing my cook. Would you like to see what's on the menu?"

"Sure," Ari and Darica said in unison as they followed Rolanda into the kitchen.

Nolan was still standing in the same spot looking pitiful and nursing a drink. He was on his way over to us but was stopped by a woman in a form-fitting black dress that hugged her curves well.

Chapter Thirteen

Darica

It was always a pleasure to see my mother-in-law's best friend, Millie. Sure enough, when we got in the kitchen, she was instructing the cook on the best way to prepare the food. Millie was no stranger to pots and pans. After seeing her in action at Borderline that day she met "Mr. Neon," as everyone called Phillip, Rolanda made sure she sent her dearest friend to the finest culinary arts school in the country. She also owned and operated her own Borderline Restaurant, which was a five-star, three-story structure with 5,000 employees.

But that all went out the window when she came to Rolanda's house. Rolanda made it very clear to Millie that her staff was off-limits and she was to enjoy her visit, not call the shots. Millie was very blunt, so they often clashed when they were in the same room, but it was all in love.

Rolanda grabbed Millie's arm and escorted her into the huge dining area where Chevette and Mama C were already sitting. I hadn't seen Mama C in ages, although I spoke to her on the phone often. She was my original go-to person for recipes.

I took a seat at the head of the table close to Chevette. She had changed her hair, got color contacts, and made a couple of changes to her wardrobe. She looked great. I reached out my hand to squeeze hers when I realized

I had grabbed the wrong cell phone. The new one was a Galaxy that was identical to Dolan's. I didn't know if he knew I had his phone, but I was sure he needed it. I scanned the room, but he was nowhere to be found.

I got up to look for him when I saw Nuni walk in. As usual, he was dressed to the nines, making us all look like peasants.

"Happy birthday, girlfriend!" he yelled.

"Hey, love. You look amazing."

"Of course, I do," he replied arrogantly as he handed me a gift.

I mingled with the rest of my guests and was having a good time, but the fact that I was missing my cell phone was looming over me, and I wasn't going to rest until I got it. It was hard to believe Dolan got this past my radar. I managed to avoid birthday parties for years. For the five years we were married, I told him I didn't want anything special, just something to eat and maybe a cupcake with a candle on it, and that was exactly what he did. We would have a good time, just the two of us, and sometimes April, hitting a restaurant, club, or bar and celebrating until the crack of dawn.

I could tolerate the birthdays. It was the parties I hated. It seemed like every birthday that I was linked to a party, something crazy would follow. On the day I was born, Mama started bleeding and almost died having me. If that wasn't enough, I broke my leg right after my friends went home on my sixth birthday. On my tenth, my crush came to my celebration at a local pizza parlor and told me I was the ugliest girl in the world.

I thought the curse was broken on my sixteenth, but cheerleader tryouts happened to be that day, and I was chosen—and told it was a mistake almost instantly. I told Mama to take back everything for the party she was planning. She hadn't even given it yet, and I'd already gotten kicked off the cheerleading squad. Right then and there, I knew I would never want another birthday party again.

When I found out that Dolan had given me this surprise party, something that I had no control over, I was completely spooked, and I was horrified to see what tonight would bring me. For that reason, I made it a point to scope out everything that was going down. I combed every guest, staff person, nook, cranny, and floor. I didn't know if my fate was going to be an argument or a slip and fall. I just knew that it was inevitable that something bad was going to happen.

I looked over at Nolan, who was standing in a crowd of women. He looked good, and I was immediately transported to those three lovely days we spent trying to conceive. I hated myself for thinking about being under him once again and cursed my insides for producing wetness between my thighs. He looked like he was trying to come up with an excuse to break away from his fans, probably so he could make a beeline to me and explain why he bought me such expensive birthday gifts. What the hell was he thinking? Not only did he purchase a diamond necklace, but he also bought me a Givenchy evening gown. I mean, where the hell was I supposed to wear them—out on a date with my husband? I put that shit far back in the closet and hoped like hell that Dolan wouldn't find them. As much as I wanted to give Nolan's ass a piece of my mind, I knew now was not the time. I scanned the room and saw my husband talking to a vivacious woman in a black dress and decided to make them my priority.

From the back, she looked breathtaking, and she was making all the gestures that told me she was flirting with my man. I hoped that the front of her face looked like a witch, so I would feel some relief that he seemed to be so comfortable talking to her. He had to have sensed me because he turned around, nodded at me, and excused himself before heading in my direction.

"Are you enjoying yourself, baby?" he smiled.

"Of course," I lied. "It looks like you're having a ball."

"Aww, baby. I was just mingling. She has nothing on you," he said as he ushered me back toward the dining area.

"Did you know that I have your—" I said before a piercing voice shattered the room.

"Greeeegggg!" she screeched.

Rolanda

This bitch really had me twisted. I already told her family functions were not a place for her personal bull-shit, but she insisted on coming with that drama. She had a baby on her hip and her mother in tow as she walked into the dining room screaming like a banshee.

"He's not here," I told her.

"Well, where is he? If this bitch is here, he can't be too far behind," Rella said as she pointed at Chevette.

"Who you calling a bitch?" said Chevette.

"If the shoe fits, wear it," Rella said as she put her hand on her hip and popped her gum.

"You know what?" Chevette said as she stood up. "You can get it. I'm tired of you disrespecting me and calling me out of my name. You slept with my husband and had a so-called baby by him. You need to take her ugly ass back and find out who her real daddy is because she don't look nothing like Greg."

"Well, all right then." Nuni snapped his fingers in a zigzag motion.

I was all set to jump in, but Mama C stopped me, letting me know that for the first time in her life, Chevette had this one.

"Who the hell are you talking to?" Rella asked.

"Your dumb ass is the only one I see in here who's laying up with a married man. But I can't blame you. You're just doing what comes naturally. I blame his thirsty ass as much as you."

"You just mad 'cause I got your man."

"You can have him. I'm scared I might catch something because your crusty ass look like you don't bathe or take care of your hygiene. Look at your hair and how you're dressed. You knew you were coming to a formal event. That busted-down wig and those ashy knees are a no-no. Clearly, you don't care about yourself, and I feel sorry for that baby."

Rella looked down at herself, and for the first time, questioned her looks. "Tell Greg he need to come see his daughter," she answered and walked back out.

"I'm proud of you," Mama C smiled.

"Me too." Millie laughed. "She said tell Greg like she needed you to relay the message. What's wrong? He's not communicating with her?"

"I wouldn't know. I've been staying here and getting myself together. I don't have time for this shit."

"Good for you," Mama C said as she gave her a high five. "I wish more wives would stand their ground."

Darica

I laughed my ass off when I saw my girl flip the script on Rella's trifling ass. Maybe she was the bad luck that the birthday curse brought me. As much as I wanted that to be true, however, I knew it was far from it. The curse was always terrible, and it always directly affected me.

What most people didn't know, and they would never hear from me, was that the birthday curse morphed into the most traumatic experience of my life. Mama didn't listen to me the day I got rejected from the cheerleading squad. She went right on with her party plans, hoping that the festivities would cheer me up. I was on pins and needles the entire time until I convinced myself that I already had my stroke of bad luck for the day, and it couldn't possibly get any worse.

How wrong I was.

When the party was over, my friend Beulah was stranded because her mother's car wouldn't start, and the only way we were going to be able to clean up and get any rest was if someone took her home. Since most of my friends' parents had already picked them up, the only person left to drive her was Ben. I jumped in the car, so she wouldn't feel like she was riding with a stranger.

Beulah only lived about fifteen minutes away, so I figured we'd be back in thirty minutes, which meant I would be back in time to help my mother clean up and eventually climb into bed with a huge piece of leftover birthday cake. We dropped Beulah off without a hitch, but on the way home, Ben took a detour. Before I could say anything, he started explaining.

"I need to make a quick stop," he said.

"Can't you go later?" I whined.

"No. I need to do it now."

I had a sick feeling in the pit of my stomach, but I sat back in my seat for the ride. Ben parked the car in the alley and went into a beat-up, dilapidated house not too far from where the car was. I saw all kinds of people running in and out. People who looked like zombies, some with Afros, mismatched shoes, no shoes, some in their pajamas, and some that looked like they hadn't taken a bath in weeks.

He was taking a long time to come out, but I was scared to look for him. I cowered in my seat, hoping no one would notice I was in the car. I almost breathed a sigh of relief when someone snatched the door open— until I saw it wasn't Ben.

"Hey, cutie. You been here for a long time. I guess your daddy forgot about you. You want me to escort you in to look for him?"

"No, thank you," I said.

"Suit yourself," he answered but refused to go away.

"Can you close the door?" I asked.

"Say please," he demanded.

"Please," I obeyed. He licked his lips like he was about to get something tasty.

"I bet you'd like it if I pleased you."

"No, sir," I told him, hoping he would leave. But he had a thirsty look on his face. "Please don't hurt me," I pleaded.

"It won't hurt at all." He winked as he yanked my dress up and pulled my panties to the side.

"Please, no," I cried.

"Shut the fuck up," he said as he placed what felt like a warm, fleshy pipe at my entrance and attempted to push himself inside me.

"Oh my God!" I screamed. "That hurts."

"Shut up, bitch! You ain't no virgin!" he yelled as he placed his large hand over my mouth. "But you're tight as hell."

I started squirming and beating him for dear life, but he didn't flinch. I tried to bite him, but the flatness of his chest made my teeth slip off. I needed to bite into something that would hurt him, so I pretended I wanted to pull him in for a kiss.

"I knew you wanted it." He smiled as he closed his eyes and brought his face to me. I licked his earlobe and wanted to puke, but I got him to stop humping me, so I knew I had an advantage. Then I bit his ear so hard. I thought I was going to end up with a bloody chunk of it in my mouth.

"Aaaaaaaah, little bitch!" he yelled as he stood up to grab his ear. I braced myself for his next move, almost sure he would kill me but happy for the victory of not getting raped.

Ben pulled him off me and looked at me in horror.

"What did you do?" he said to my attacker.

"That bitch asked for it," he told Ben while still holding his ear and running to his car.

"What have I done?" Ben repeated over and over as I covered my naked body. We heard sirens and police cars coming from everywhere. The officers started grabbing people out of the crack house left and right.

"Who did this to you?" a female officer asked. All I could do was point out the window. *"Don't worry. We'll make sure he pays."* She looked at Ben in disgust.

"He didn't do it," I protested. But no one would listen to me describe the real assailant.

Dolan

I didn't know who invited Cee's ass to the party, but what I did know was I wanted to get her the hell out. She thought she was cute prancing in my wife's party trying to start some shit, but I didn't have time for anyone's shenanigans, especially after I just got rid of Miko's ass. I just got my wife back and would be damned if I let anyone fuck it up for me.

I had one of the guards quietly escort her out and enlisted a few more to make sure she didn't get back up in here. Running into her was an unexpected fluke, and her coming to the house was a mishap that I didn't plan to allow again.

With that mission accomplished, I pulled out my cell phone. It was ringing off the hook all day with all kinds of text messages and calls. I usually didn't get as many as two calls a day and hardly any text messages. If I didn't know any better, I would have thought I picked up my wife's phone instead of my own.

I opened up my messages and saw that there were about five; plus, there were about three voicemail messages. Just from looking at the texts, I could tell I had my wife's phone. April had texted her that she would be late for the party with her silly self. She was so stuck on herself; she didn't think about the fact that her text might ruin the surprise.

There was a phone number from a free clinic in Nebraska. Darica and I had no secrets, so I pushed the button for her visual voicemail and got the shock of my life.

Nolan

The look on Dolan's face when he saw Cee, aka, Carlena, was priceless. Back in the day when he fucked her to get back at Miko, his weak ass didn't count on falling in love with her, but she popped, locked, and dropped it on him so good he was like putty in her hands.

Now, me, I learned early on that the best thing to do was hit it and quit it, but my brother always liked to bite off more than he could chew. The amount of time and effort he put into relationships, only to see them fail, pissed me off. If you were gonna have a woman, she better not only be a bad bitch but a special one. He and Cee only stayed together until they graduated high school. A lot of people thought they were going to get married, but something happened, and they broke up. She tried a couple of times to get back with him, but he wasn't feeling her. I wondered what was going on with them now. I knew she came for something, but for what, I did not know.

I planned to find out, though, just as soon as I got rid of Ari's ass. I didn't trust her since the time she went ballistic and confronted Sheila. We all know how that ended. She knew now that she and I would never be together, but I figured that still wouldn't stop her from spilling the beans to Darica sooner or later.

Truth be told, if Mom hadn't jumped the gun and invited her into the kitchen, I would have had security escort her ass out a long time ago. She knew she had no business at the party.

Darica

"About damn time," I fussed at April with my hand on my hip.

"Don't cuss at me, chica. I was stuck in the mall. I had to get you the perfect gift."

"It better be a Bentley, as long as you took."

"Shit, if it was a Bentley, I would have never made it here. I would've kept it for myself and got your ass something else."

"Quit playing. You know how I hate parties. God knows I needed you a long time ago. Why did you let Dolan do this after I told you about the curse?"

"I barely found out about it myself; plus, I tried to call your fast ass, but I guess you're not answering calls, texts, or voicemails."

"I don't have my phone. I accidentally took Dolan's."

"Oh shit. I told you about letting a man hold your phone."

"Up until now, it's worked out for us. I haven't found anything on his phone, and he hasn't found anything on mine."

"Be careful, chica. There's a first time for everything."

I grabbed April's hand and sat her down beside me, then looked at the empty seat on my right. I was about to get nervous until I saw Dolan walk in. I was so relieved when he sat down beside me, as dinner was being served. It smelled delicious, and I dived in as soon as I got my food. The whole time I was eating, Dolan kept looking at me like he wanted to say something. He was only able to contain himself long enough for us to eat.

"I have an announcement to make," he said as he stood up and hit his knife on a wineglass. "My beautiful wife is apparently too embarrassed to say it, but the fact that she left me her phone shows me that, in addition to having a great sense of humor, she's always full of surprises. Don't worry, baby. I know you're too shy to do this yourself. I take great pleasure in making this announcement to all of our family and friends. We're expecting a baby."

I was so horrified; I could barely hear everyone congratulating me. I guess Dolan checked my visual voicemail, which I never bothered to lock, and heard a message from my obstetrician. Aside from wishing I had followed April's advice and locked my phone, I looked up and saw a face I hadn't seen in years—the man that had attacked me in Ben's car. I never knew what became of him until, one day, I saw him on TV. Then I knew the reason why the officer arrested Ben, and my attacker got off scot-free.

It turned out he was the Welterweight champion of the world, in the wrong place at the wrong time in the car with his brother who was buying crack when he saw me.

He was at his prime and felt like he could have anything he wanted at the time. So he walked over to Ben's car, thinking I was a potential groupie who would recognize him as the champ and do whatever he asked. I didn't think he was counting on damn near raping me, but that was exactly how it went down.

Suddenly, the bile rising in my throat became more important than the champ, and I got up, put my hand over my mouth, and ran to the nearest bathroom as fast as I could.

"I remember morning sickness," I heard someone say.

Chapter Fourteen

Nolan

When Dolan made that announcement, it was one of the proudest moments of my life because it meant I was officially a daddy. My chest felt like it puffed out ten inches, and I wanted to beat on it like Tarzan. Mina would pick this moment to be blowing up my phone, but I was so done with her, it wasn't even funny. I turned my phone off and stood up.

I didn't care that Evette had just walked in or that the former Welterweight champion of the world came to talk business with my brother. I was just glad that he was going to keep him busy for a while. When Dolan told April to follow Darica, I told her, "I got this."

April eyed me seductively. I hadn't seen her since the day I used her to get Darica's phone number, but I knew she still had the hots for me. I wondered how she'd feel if she knew that I was in love with her best friend. Would she hate me? Would she hate Darica, thinking she seduced me, or would she embrace it and try to help us? On any other day, I would've been anxious to find out, but the most important thing to me at the moment was making it to the bathroom to hold Darica's hair out of her face.

I assumed she would go into the nearest guest bathroom, which was right next to the dining area. But when I got there, I didn't find her anywhere. I started walking around the huge house looking for her, but she was nowhere to be found.

Evette

I had tried to call Daddy to tell him I had changed my mind about getting in on his business deal, but he didn't answer the phone, so I came to the party where he was at. When I walked into the house and heard Nolan's brother making the announcement, I couldn't believe my ears. The brother was saying that his wife was pregnant, and, somehow, I knew Nolan had finally done the unthinkable. After all the bitches he had fucked, this shit right here took the cake. I had just paid Mina off and sent her ass out of town, and like a good little soldier, she complied. But this Darica bitch was another story, and if she was pregnant by Nolan, I knew she had to go too. His actions showed me he was already in love with her, but that child would take him over the deep end, and there would be no more us. We could've already had a baby if he hadn't worn those condoms and kept pulling out.

The fucked-up part about it was that she was his brother's wife, and I knew damn well that wasn't jumping off. I didn't know exactly what to do with her, but I had a couple of ideas. I followed him like a toddler waiting for him to find her, so I could find out what I needed to know. I didn't know what I would do, but I was sure I would hurt her real badly if she said it was his child.

Carlena

Dolan had me escorted out, but I paid security and walked back in just in time to hear the announcement. I wanted to slice that bitch's head off. After all the years I had put into getting Dolan back, he went and married that bitch and tried to give her a baby, when he wouldn't even let me get off birth control.

The only way Darica could be pregnant was if Dolan's sperm count went up, or if she cheated with another man. And since I had no way of being sure, I was going to have to get rid of the bitch the best way I knew how.

Darica

Carlena came from out of nowhere, and at first, I wanted to ask her why she was at my party. She was a big help at the clinic where I was trying to conceive, but the look on her face now was nothing like the sweet one I was used to. I didn't know her well enough to ask her to come, and I couldn't blame her invite on my mother-in-law because she didn't even know that we were going to that clinic. Even if she did, I doubt she would invite my counselor over for my birthday. I didn't think that Dolan did it because he didn't even feel she was close enough for us to invite her to lunch, so it was awkward for her to be at such an intimate event. And I certainly didn't count on Nolan inviting her because I didn't think they hit it off like that either.

When she shoved me into the closet, I was more than shocked. I knew she was off when she wound duct tape around my mouth and arms and put a sharp knife into my back.

Carlena

"Okay, bitch. I'm going to talk, and you're going to listen. If you make one move to alert anyone that we're

in here, I'm going to fillet your ass. Do you understand?"
Darica nodded, knowing I meant business. "Good girl.
Now, let me bring you up to speed. I've been fucking
Dolan off and on for years." I paused for effect and
watched her reaction. She shook her head, and I saw
tears in her eyes. I went on with my story. "I was his first
love, so that shows you where you are on the totem pole.
That baby he says he wants so badly means nothing to
him. He is just playing you until he can make the divorce
happen. Since you are technically in the way, I'm going
to help him along. We already know he can't give you a
baby, so it's safe to say that you fucked someone else to
get it. Am I correct?"

She gave me the look of death, so I kept on talking.
"It's fine if you don't want to talk, but let me warn you
that I know the treatments didn't work. You can't tell that
to your husband, now, can you? It seems to me like the
only thing left for you to do is leave, so Dolan and I can
be happy."

She shook her head no at that point, and I knew what
I had to do.

Dolan

I thought the police would never arrive, so I was
somewhat relieved when a detective finally walked in.
We'd been looking for Darica in the huge house for what
seemed like forever, and when we didn't find her, we
didn't know what to think. April was frantic, my mother
was hyperventilating, and everyone else was so nervous
that they could barely move.

"Hello, Mr. Rogiers, I'm Detective Hughes," he addressed
my brother.

"Are you here about my wife?" I asked.

"No. I'm here to question Nolan Rogiers about the death of Sheila Carter, the disappearance of Essence Jackson, and Wilhemina Jones, a coworker, a prostitute, and a friend of his that were all last seen with him, all having relations with him, and all missing."

I opened the door wider to allow Detective Hughes inside my parents' home. My brother Nolan was looking like the cat that ate the canary, an indication that he'd once again found himself in trouble. I wasn't concerned about him or that dumb-ass detective. Right now, all I cared about was my wife.

I excused myself to a nearby guest room and sat down to call her again. This time she answered on the first ring, sniffled like she was crying and whimpered like a baby.

"It's okay, baby. I know you're overwhelmed by the party, the announcement, and the fact you wanted to tell me yourself that you were pregnant. I know your first instinct is always to run, but you don't have to do that anymore. Whatever you're going through, we're going to work it out together. We finally have our family. Aren't you excited?"

She didn't answer, but I knew she was just as excited as I was, and I knew she'd eventually give in and agree.

"Ummmm," she moaned inaudibly.

"Shhhhh," I hushed her. "It's time to stop running. If you trust that we're going to happy, that all our dreams are about to come true, and that this is the start of the rest of our lives, hang up this phone and come to me. I'm in the front guest room. I'll be waiting for you."

The phone hung up, almost instantaneously, and I was happy knowing that my wife was on her way and all the drama would soon be behind us.

Hopefully, my brother would be a distant memory as well once the detective spoke to him, that is, and it just might end with him being arrested. That would take him out of the picture, and my previous concerns regarding his obsession with my wife would no longer be an issue. Nevertheless, it would all take a back burner to my current situation which was first and foremost, my future with my family.

I made sure the door was unlocked, took my suit coat off, lay down on the queen-sized bed, and cracked my first genuine grin in ages. I was about to be a daddy.

Darica

I couldn't believe Dolan betrayed me with such a crazy bitch, but when I felt the sharp knife pierce my stomach, I knew she was serious. The wound was so deep that in a matter of seconds, I was too weak to move. I couldn't call out with the duct tape on my mouth, so I resolved myself to the fact that I would bleed out and feared for the life of my unborn child more than my own.

I listened to Dolan and Nolan frantically looking for me and making phone calls from the other side of the door. They'd called the police and continued to search for me, and I was right there under their noses the whole time. I imagined the expression on their faces when I was finally found dead in the closet. I also thought about the humiliation they'd suffer when the true story was revealed.

Flashbacks of my childhood and wedding, flashbacks of Mama, Daddy, Ben, April, Nuni, Nolan, Dolan, and my unborn child invaded my thoughts as I drifted into darkness, and suddenly, I hated myself for every choice I had made, including coming to this godforsaken party.

The ringing phone startled me. I pushed the send key and listened to my husband ramble on about what he thought was the matter. He was so busy ranting that he didn't notice I wasn't answering his questions. I was still too weak to remove the duct tape secured around my mouth, but his words prompted me to discard what I was thinking about just seconds ago when I was contemplating death.

I wanted to tell him that I was frantically fighting for my life and that I didn't know if I'd ever make it to that guestroom, but the call got disconnected. I realized he must've thought I hung up so that I could follow his orders, and he was expecting me to show up.

I went into survival mode, tried to muster up some strength to get to safety, which I was determined to do even if it took every ounce of energy I had. A pool of blood, my blood, surrounded me, but it didn't stop me from getting that tape off my mouth.

Neither one of us was perfect. We'd been through the fire, but we weren't any worse for the wear. We'd managed to do something right, and accomplished the unthinkable. For that, we *deserved* to be parents. I knew right then and there it was going to take more than trifling-ass Carlena to stop that from happening because, from this day forward, no problem would ever be greater than us.

Feeling a little shaky, I called him back and told him where I was. It didn't take him long to find me. As he opened the closet door, he looked at me in disbelief. The moment I looked into his eyes, I saw our future. I saw myself in the hospital recovering from my injuries. I saw myself in labor getting ready to have our baby. I saw the family we were always destined to be . . . changing diapers, preparing bottles, and taking our son to preschool. It was right then and there that I knew nothing would ever break us. We were Rogiers, and the Rogiers were always resilient. That's just the way it was.

It didn't matter who fathered our child or how the child was conceived. The only thing that did matter was it would grow up loved, cared for, and nurtured in just the right way. Everything else would fall in place.

"We're going to get through this, and we're going to be great parents," Dolan assured me.

"No doubt," I nodded, believing every word.

The End